MONGOLLEN
AND OTHER
STORIES

BY

ALAN GIBBINS

Grosvenor House
Publishing Limited

The right of Alan Gibbins to be identified as the author of this
work has been asserted in accordance with Section 78
of the Copyright, Designs and Patents Act 1988

The book cover picture is copyright to Alan Gibbins

This book is published by
Grosvenor House Publishing Ltd
28-30 High Street, Guildford, Surrey, GU1 3EL.
www.grosvenorhousepublishing.co.uk

A CIP record for this book
is available from the British Library

ISBN 978-1-78623-006-5

Dedication

To my late dear wife Kathleen
and
To our daughter Susan.

Acknowledgements

John and Carol Young for their encouragement
and illustrations.

Tamsin of Grosvenor House Publishing for
her invaluable guidance.

To Wendy
from
Alan Gittins

Contents

MONGOLLEN

PART 1

Let me introduce to you a small country with a problem.

The country is Mongollen, little heard of and unknown to most, save for the neighbouring country of Inner Mongolia, an autonomous region of China, whose influence is overriding.

In contrast to its neighbours Mongollen enjoys a mildish, temperate climate, brought about by the generous sized hills which shelter it from the more extremes in weather in those parts and as such is fortunate indeed. For example, in the Inner Mongolian capital of Hohhot, a matter of 50 miles north of the Mongollen border, summer can be warm but short (say 2 or 3 months from July, when temperatures tend to be 16 to 27 centigrade, although peaks of 30 are not unknown). This is considerably improved on in Mongollen, first in the much longer summer season, and in the less rigorous winter months when Hohhot can average -12 through November to January, and -1 to +9 by April. These values are significantly bettered in Mongollen and the skies are likely to be sunny with high pressure dominating. Rainfall is generally moderate – up to 15 inches annually.

Mongollen is an Oligarchy, governed by the family O'Gollens of Irish extraction. Patrick O'Gollen 1st was the self-anointed King back in the early 1800's, Cogollen is the capital, Gollenese the people. How the Irish came here in the mists of time is a mystery which cannot be ascribed to the Potato Famine in Ireland from 1844 on which led to mass emigration westwards, but not eastwards so far as is known. In any event it seems likely that the Irish incursion pre dates that as history in the region records pre blight potatoes being grown, presumably introduced by the Irish who brought with them a staple in their accustomed diet, and a feed for livestock.

It is interesting to speculate as to the manner of their welcome by the Inner Mongolians and, more importantly, the Chinese.

There is a similarity here to the settling in 1865 by the Welsh emigrants to Patagonia in southern Argentina. This was brought about with the full agreement of the Argentine Government who allowed the settlement of the Chubut valley by the Welsh, driven to this by the desire not to be subsumed by the English culture which threatened their way of life. This has been successfully achieved in Y Wladfa, the Welsh colony. Today we see a population of 120000 in the largest town of Trelew, and probably ½ million overall. A small proportion are of purely Welsh origin, but at least ½ have Welsh blood in their veins, and there is a strong sense of Welsh roots throughout. Patagonian Welsh is the dialect spoken by a substantial part of the population.

The Irish story echoes the Welsh but in fact preceded it, so it can be taken to have encouraged the Welsh settlement in South America. In the same way the Mongollen enterprise can surely be ascribed to the example of the Quakers on the Mayflower in their heroic adventure in 1620 to colonise the Eastern seaboard of the New World. What, one wonders, does this say about the English who precipitated 3 evacuations prompted for cultural reasons?

It seems that the Irish felt much the same as the Welsh in that their identity could be stripped over time by the English influences, and as an alternative to the more drastic measures to come with the Troubles (which have gone on to the recent past) possibly the O'Gollens and their kith and kin felt it worthwhile to make overtures to the Chinese with a view to establishing an Irish conclave south of Inner Mongolia. There is no evidence of a formal agreement by the Chinese to this now de facto situation, but nor has there been any indication of objection, and relations, although not close are friendly.

Of course it must be said that the O'Gollen's incursion was a long time before Mao Tse Tung's era and the rather surprising mixture now of Capitalism and Communism which seems successful. In the early 1800's China was a tangled web of disparate regions and it is likely that at that time the arrival of an Irish dimension was barely noticed.

And so the O'Gollens have been accepted, and more surprisingly, the oligarchy became a Kingdom. I think that tacit acceptance by the Chinese is due to their sense of humour which takes a perverse pleasure in seeing the absolute contradiction between the largest Communist State and the smallest Kingdom on the planet living in harmony side by side. I think they also take pleasure in cocking a snook at the English who have caused them difficulties over the years, as with the Welsh and the Irish.

As with most Irish families the O'Gollens are a large brood; indeed a goodly number of the population of Mongollen are named O'Gollen and speak a dialect of Mongolese/Gaelic largely unintelligible to their neighbours, particularly when spiked with a plethora of Begorrahs which is the Irish way of stressing the importance of their point.

This does cause some difficulties in communication with Inner Mongolia and China, but as King Patrick suggested, it may be too taxing for the Gollenese to learn Mandarin, and as interaction with immediate neighbours was relatively infrequent was not considered a great trial.

Currently we now see a King Patrick 3rd aged about 50 with a considerable following of Princes and Princesses. His number one son is named Seamus and so we see the mould being broken, at least in so far as the Monarch's name is concerned, but it is a good Irish name and is welcomed as such.

I won't go into the immediate family of O'Gollen by name; suffice it to say that the family is so extended that the Oligarchy is assured for the foreseeable future. Much though depends on their ability to find a solution to the PROBLEM.

I said at the outset that this was a small country, but it has grown since inception. To the extent that at the last census numbers came out around 500000 or so souls, half of whom lived in the capital Cogollen and its surrounds, the rest in scattered villages and small towns.

At the heart of the country lies Lake Titigollen, beautifully situated in the valley below the protective hills. Round about is good agricultural land providing grazing for sheep and cattle, and arable land whose main crops are wheat, potatoes (an Irish speciality of course) vegetables and most importantly for Mongollen, the oats and barley destined to provide the life enhancing brown porter devised by the Irish in the distant past. This is spiked up to a large degree with an Inner Mongolian concoction which is known as mare's milk wine or airag which defies most taste buds and the overall result can lead to the mother and father of a hangover. This, despite the fact that airag is not fiercely alcoholic by itself, but when injected into the black stuff, results in a formidable mixture. Fortuitously the likely outcome seems to escape most Gollenese whose ancestry has long been famous for the ability to make light of strong liquor, a trait echoed in the fabled Irish capacity in this area.

To a large extent the country is self-sufficient and agricultural produce forms 90% of GDP. The rest comes from various articles of native art, producing pottery etc. (much of which takes the form of ceramic Lephrechauns doing what Lephrechauns do). It is surprising that some of the export items from Mongollen can command good prices in the more sophisticated countries in the West, and this can only be explained by the fact that few collectors have ever heard of Mongollen, and so, to possess an item marked "a present from Mongollen" initiates unbounded interest in those lucky enough to have secured it.

This, incidentally, will have been difficult to bring about because the ins and outs of Import/Export finance is a closed book to the Gollenese and is largely accomplished by a system of barter and haggling. In this the Gollenese are a superior force to most. Indeed it is true that the Moroccon Souk traders have expressed their admiration for their haggling expertise, which came to their notice when one of their number took a wrong flight, intending to go from Marrakesh to Delhi (to visit family members) and ended up in Hohhot at the time of a Trade Fair where Mongollen had an exhibition of its native art. This did not impress the visitor so much as the ability to close out a sale in the most advantageous manner for the Mongollen sales team, whether by barter or hard cash, simply by refusing to meet anyone half or even 9/10th way. It was subsequently agreed that a delegation from Marrakesh should visit Mongollen to sharpen their technique.

My experience of shopping in Marrakesh Souks is a nightmare which should not be heightened further but the wish of the Moroccons to learn more underlines the expertise the Gollenese possess in this system of trading.

All is well in Mongollen then?

No, I am afraid not.

Lake Titigollen is the trouble. Over many years the waters in this tranquil spot have been polluted to a high degree by effluent emanating from livestock and from mankind. It is fair to say that over many decades Lake Titigollen has been an en-suite toilet with absolutely no system of flushing.

It reached the stage whereby the lake was at its highest level, and it would be a very short time before its dangerous toxic waters washed over the verdant plains surrounding. The result was highly predictable, leading, as it surely would, to the ruination of the arable land over a large part of the plains so beneficial to the well-being of the country. This has provided the main subject of debate throughout the Government comprised in the main by the O'Gollen family, although in fairness there has been of late some move on the part of the Royals to introduce a more representative body. To this end King Patrick has appointed a few of the common herd to the Government benches. There is of course no Opposition Bench. Needless to say the appointees have been well vetted by the MON GSS and MON GPF (Secret Service and Police Force)

The pollution reached the point a long time ago when fresh water fish ceased to be part of the diet of the Gollenese and this has resulted in a serious diminution in the little grey cells of even the cleverest Mongollen citizens. In all honesty this was a small bunch anyway. Mental capacity was never much prized, preference being in the high regard held for manly (and womanly) physique, and of abilities in the Irish tradition of pugilism and child conception.

Solutions to the problem were not coming forward readily, and so King Patrick 3rd felt he must bring to bear his God given right to take the lead.

As to this his first thought was a recollection of sending his No 1 son Prince Seamus to the Inner Mongolian University in Hohhot on a much vaunted educational trip with nothing really in mind as an outcome. Up to date such an outcome had been fully realised. Nevertheless the intent to broaden the mind of the Prince was much admired. With this recollection The King decided that he would place the solution to the problem in the hands of Prince Seamus, then a stripling of 20 or so years.

During his curtailed stay at the seat of learning it should be said that the Prince did further his education in a number of ways, attending most of the convivial meetings in the Uni bar where he met a great number of extremely attractive female students who were little interested in his brain but overwhelmed by his Mongollen machoism which sprung from his Irish descent. This had the evident traces of an Errol Flynn (do I hear those of my younger readers muttering Errol who?) Surely with a name like that must be of the clan.

However the very evident tendency to skip serious lectures led to the realisation by the Tutors that they were banging their heads against a brick wall. This was hurting and so the curtailment mentioned was brought about by University authorities.

However Prince Seamus had, since his outside education, adopted a pensive visage as he moved amongst the people, eschewing the usual physical nature of his instincts, and impressing with his cerebral view of the world at large, and his ordained space within it. As behoves an educated man.

But now his father had put him in a spot which called for rather more than a pensive visage, and the Prince admitted to himself that he was at a loss to know how to proceed.

One particular mathematical poser was etched (ever so slightly) in his memory of his sojourn at the seat of learning. This concerned the schoolboy teaser relating to filling a bathtub with two taps turned fully on, and with the bathtub plug out, and the time which it would take to accomplish this.

The actual problem is posed thus:

If it takes 15 minutes to fill a bathtub with water, plug in and two taps full on, and it takes 20 minutes for the bathtub to empty (taps off and plug out) how long will it take to fill with two taps full on and the plug out.

We all know that 1 hour is the accepted answer, assuming fill and empty rates are constant, viz:

Fill rate 1/15 per minute

Empty rate 1/20 per minute

Net rate 1/15 - 1/20 = 1/60 per minute – a difficult concept to grasp most will agree.

So bathtub will fill in 1 hour in these circumstances.

Prince Seamus caused consternation when he expressed disagreement when this finding was being dealt with by an eminent Professor of Fluid Mechanics. First because Seamus was actually present at a real lecture, and secondly that he had stayed awake long enough after a heavy night to absorb the equation.

His reason to believe that the bathtub would never fill completely was based on the fallacy implicit in the equation that no regard should be had to the presence (certainly in most bathtubs in his experience at University – he had no experience in Mongollen where bathtubs were unknown) of an over flow system.

This recollection of his ever so slight brush with the mysteries of Fluid Mechanics reminded him that he had been sufficiently interested to pursue the question further, when he found that the full behaviour in bathtubs with taps on and off, and with plugs in and out, was better modelled using Bernoulli's equation. This of course was propounded in the 1700's by Danielle Bernoulli, a famous scientist of that era. With little expectation of following the reasoning the Prince secured a copy of the Equation which he brought home with him on expulsion. His favourite amusement had been since was to put this to family and friends to their utter bemusement, not lessened by Prince Seamus's unintelligible explanation.

Briefly his notes were as follows:
$$P1/rho \times g + V1 > 2/29 + h1 = P2/rho \times g + V2 < (29) + h2$$

Where
P1 P2 = pressures
Rho = density of water

9 = acceleration due to gravity
V1 V2=velocities
H1 h2 =heights

Bernoulli makes a few assumptions:

1 drain is a free jet, i.e. the water surface is open to the atmosphere
So P1 = P2
2 velocity of the water on the surface is negligible compared to the drainage velocity
So V1=0
He arbitrarily sets h2=0
So simplified we have
H1=V2>2(29)
Solving V2 we have
V2 = SQRT(29.h1)

Bernoulli makes one more simplifying assumption here; that the cross sectional area of the tub B is constant all the way up.

In that case V= B*h1
So we have
D=Ac*V2= Ac*SQRT9 29*B*2)

Lumping all the constants into one constant k we are left with
D= K*SQRT(V)

It has been demonstrated that it takes 20 minutes to drain a full tub so using the foregoing equation we have
dV/dt=D=k*SQRT(V)
And dv9k*SQRT9V) =dt

Bernoulli sportingly admits that the equation is surprisingly involved, but luckily we now have the ability to access the Alpha/Wolfram web site for a simple explanation. I do not recommend it because herein lies the path to madness. Suffice it to say that Bernoulli concludes that with taps full on and plug out the bathtub will never fill to more than 5/6th of its capacity. Like Prince Seamus O'Gollen of Mongollen he came to this conclusion because he took cognisance of the fact that most bathtubs have an overflow pipe.

Notwithstanding the total bemusement the foregoing visited on Prince Seamus, just as total as on all others he afflicted in the cruel manner by which he persuaded them to visit the Equation, he nevertheless felt that somewhere in this minefield lay the answer to the Lake Titigollen problem.

Simply put he recognised that in both cases water was involved, and it was the intention of drawing it off and replacing it that was nub of the deliberations.

As to the original filling of Lake Titigollen, this had taken about 200 years of accepting the natural modest rainfall supplemented by the far more plentiful liquid (and other) toilet habits of the population. Whereas the Bernoulli Equation dealt solely with the filling, it was very clear to Prince Seamus that the first thing to be done was the emptying and the practical application of the Equation could well await that happy outcome, before it was brought to the fore in the second task. He was very conscious that this second phase must not take 200 years but felt that this was a bridge to cross when he came to it. The Equation was not going anywhere, and he resolved to ask the eminent Professor of Fluid Mechanics, with whom he had crossed swords earlier, to put his money where his mouth was as it were, and demonstrate Task 2 could be dealt with in the real world by application of the Equation on the ground. This the Prince felt was within the professional orbit of the Lecturer.

As to Task 1, this is where a well-known Irish talent inherent in the makeup of Prince Seamus, as with all of Irish descent, came to the party. Were they not known in the 18th and 19th century as the Navigators (shortened to Navvies at the time) because of their propensity for digging great canals throughout the British Isles?

So it was with a light heart and a considerable number of picks, spades and shovels that Prince Seamus enlisted the necessary labour force and set them to work on building a substantial trench from the headwaters of Lake Titigollen to the boundary with China, leaving of course the final few yards at the end as the plug to be removed at the appropriate time. Here of course Prince Seamus had regard to the findings of Isaac Newton with which he had a brief fling when at University. He was therefore fairly well briefed on the theory of gravity, which fitted in nicely with his plans, as from the headwaters of the Lake, the land ran away quite steeply, and although assuming a more gentle slope later on, Isaac would have agreed with Prince Seamus that it was quite sufficient in Gravity inducing mode to continue the descent of the outpourings, and fitted in well with the Science of Fluid Mechanics.

The question of the less soluble material running into the trench was to be dealt with by extracting it for temporary storage alongside, and in view of the rather unpleasant nature of this work, Prince Seamus called on the prison population for this necessary procedure to be rewarded by an amnesty. The number in prison involved was not great, but judged to be sufficient, and so it proved.

There was a certain disquiet (which he shared) expressed with the plan of Prince Seamus, in that it did not take account of the feelings of the Chinese neighbours who very soon must become aware of the rather unpleasant introduction of foreign matter likely to flow their way.

Admittedly this posed a real problem that Prince Seamus acknowledged would take a special argument to convince their neighbours that this could be managed and turned to their advantage.

The talent of the Irish and those Gollenese with Irish blood in their veins has been mentioned in so far as the Navigators is concerned. There is of course a further talent quite evident in past Irish accomplishments, and this is well demonstrated in their silver tongues, and the magic of their Blarney which is honoured in the stone from which it springs.

Well in advance of pulling the plugs a meeting with local representatives of the nearest Chinese local government was sought, and to this meeting King Patrick and Queen Queenie headed the Gollenese delegation, but with Prince Seamus as the main spokesperson in view of his command of the engineering project in hand. And also as a result of his astonishing success of blandishments to scores of Inner Mongolian maidens at University, conducted in their own language so closely linked to the Mandarin spoken in China proper. This ability to put over the finer points of the PROBLEM in language understood by the Chinese was crucial but it was recognised of course, that Chinese government officials, even at a local level, would pose a much bigger nut to crack.

As it happened the Chinese had become aware of the activity over the border, and not liking what they heard and saw, local Government called in more senior of the nation's leaders in the belief that all the activity of digging etc. could only mean that the Gollenese were building fortifications from which they intended to launch a surprise attack on their peaceful neighbour. Incredible as this appeared on the face of it, considering the huge gulf between the two in military might (it was registered as NIL for Mongollen) the possibility was not dismissed out of hand. This was because rumours of the bellicosity of the Irish in the past were not discounted, although the reasons which would precipitate a return to those days escaped the Chinese.

With no little incredulity the Chinese Foreign Secretary and his team journeyed to Cogollen to learn of the Gollenese intentions. In their turn the suspicions of the Chinese as to motive were viewed by King Patrick and his advisors with great hilarity, and this produced an atmosphere akin to bonhomie. This was regarded by the opposite numbers as a good starting point for fruitful discussion after the nature of the Gollenese problem was fully explained, and the manner by which it was suggested it could be addressed was one in which King Patrick and his people fully intended to enlist the cooperation of their good friends from the beginning.

Of most concern to China was the effect of the effluent to be released over the border once the plug had been pulled as it were, and its ultimate destination which was likely to be the rather nice beaches of the South China Sea. At this juncture it would hardly have been surprising if all bets were off, and there were no real arguments which Prince Seamus could advance to prevent this.

However Mr Sun Yat Sang, (the Foreign Secretary) was willing to give the subject thought. He had in mind that the immediate environs his side of the border were far better equipped to deal with the waste than the Gollenese side; there was a workable system of sewerage in the area and it was not beyond the engineering skills available to him to process the waste as it came over the border although this would entail a substantial extension of piping, water purification plant etc. Beyond this of course was the future strategy to avoid a build-up of the old problem.

To do this it would be necessary to bring Mongollen up to date in the sewerage world; to plumb in every home and business place and to clean up their act in all aspects for the new order.

The plan though did not stop at that. In his exploration of Mongollen he had been very taken with much of its charm and its potential as a tourist trap had not escaped him. There were substantial mountains at the northern extremity running down to more gentle hills and then on to the plains, and so to Lake Titigollen. This, in its purified state would be idyllic, and when stocked with trout etc. would be paradise for the millions of anglers throughout the world.

The Foreign Secretary appointed a Committee to examine every aspect of creating the most popular resort in the Far East which worked diligently for a month or two. They came up with a plan, first to build the necessary infrastructure providing decent roads, access to power through gas and oil and electric sources in China.Then to build 4 & 5 star hotels, Casinos, Golf courses, Restaurants, Bars, Petrol stations and all the cornucopia of the hedonistic lifestyle, and this would spread out of the Capital to the gentle hills in the north. Over the border with Inner Mongolia there were two or three ski slopes close to Hohhot which could be accessed by tourists. In due time the Committee felt such a Resort would become the equal of Monte Carlo and Las Vegas. They were though conscious that one thing was lacking. There was no plan for a beach. In their view it was essential that a resort should have a seaside.

So a revolutionary scheme was suggested. The trench built in Mongollen should be extended into China, dug out to receive all the spoil stored at the side, and over laid with a substantial thickness of tarmac. This would become a four lane highway to the coast where development would be competitive with the French Riviera, and certainly eclipse the English Riviera at Torquay. Although rightfully in China, it would be known as the Gollenese Riviera.

Here, dear reader, you may feel the urge to consult the world Atlas to explore the geographic realities of what is suggested here. I would ask that you do not follow that path, and accept that the beaches on the South China Sea are all they are cracked up to be in this narrative, and to believe that the four lane highway linking Shangri Las Vegas (for that will be the name of the new Resort in Mongollen) to the Gollenese Riviera will provide easy access in a short time by car and coach. After all this is fiction, and artistic license is expected.

The Plan received Chinese Government approval subject to a satisfactory agreement with Mongollen, firstly as to the building of the Resort, and more importantly the manner of funding the considerable expense. It is hardly likely that the Chinese interest would be altruistic. Costs must be met although it was quite evident that this could not be done in the short term from Gollenese coffers which were virtually non-existent. Recovery of costs was a first step, but beyond that it was to be expected that the scheme should provide a healthy income for the Chinese to give great satisfaction to their best exponents of recently acquired Capitalistic skills.

This would be brought about by a very substantial creaming off at the top of the anticipated Tourist trade of the riches expected from 1st class Hotels, Restaurants, Bars, Casinos, Championship Golf Courses, Strip Clubs, Lap dancing Clubs et al. Some of these latter entertainment venues were added to the plans at the last moment when it was felt that the ship should not be spoilt for a half a Yuan's worth of tar. Indeed this was very much the attitude held by the construction teams; so much so that American input was sourced in the gaming elements, and the golf courses were laid out with the speciality knowledge of a consortium of Golf architects headed by 3 well known Pro Golfers. This was a recognition of their golfing knowledge, but also of their Irish heritage.

As to the Gollenese Riviera the land on which to build the seaside paradise and the four lane highway to serve it from Mongollen was to be subject to a long lease granted by China at a rental to be negotiated further down the line when its full potential was realised.

King Patrick and his team knew full well that the rental would be substantial, but acknowledged that it could only be determined when the Riviera was up and running, and must reflect the expenditure on the separate development which was to provide first class accommodation and all amenities incorporating the usual sand and sea delights. Sensibly it was not set up in the plans to compete with the main Mongollen resort, and so much of the more extreme entertainment expected by a high percentage of tourists was not put in place on the Riviera. Here was to be a haven for those seeking a peaceful recovery from the excesses up the road. And also of course for those who were now beyond excesses – a minority certainly but one with spending power.

The plans were put before King Patrick and his advisors who received them with enthusiasm. This was before the Secretary to the Treasury in China submitted his estimation of the proportion of the income expected to be generated to give an acceptable return on capital expended. Until initial costs were covered he argued there was no profit to China and it was essential that this should be dealt with expeditiously. Until the tourist trade began to bite then returns would be on a sliding scale – hopefully upwards – until this happy point was reached. Until then the Secretary fixed the Chinese share of income at 80% and this would equate to nil in the first (hopefully short) period whilst the Tourism built up and rise to the maximum until repayment of the loans. Beyond that the division of profits would be open to negotiation. King Patrick had little optimism that the financial outcome would not be weighted in the Chinese favour, but nevertheless felt that the terms must be accepted, as he had no financial expertise to call on throughout his Kingdom. Generally it was found in Mongollen that native cunning met the bill well enough.

And so the great transformation of the Kingdom was begun, and went on a pace with no insurmountable problems. In very short order the Resort was completed to the satisfaction of all parties. Beyond the head of Lake Titigollen the sewage works were in place ready to accept the contents when Prince Seamus supervised the pulling of the plug, which he did with a fanfare, and it must be said this was difficult for the trumpeters who could not be protected from the unpleasant odour. Others at the ceremony were provided with face masks, but it is impossible to trumpet when wearing these.

The criminals earned their amnesty by their success in separating and storing the sludge for eventual burial under a good weight of tarmac which became the motorway to the coast as planned.

It then came to Task 2 in the operation to which Seamus had been giving some thought. Whilst the work carried out in the foundations of the buildings had opened up a series of fresh water springs and the volume was probably sufficient in the long term to fill the Lake, the time scale would be of the magnitude of the original filling and obviously this was not acceptable.

As an aside here I should say that the springs were a bonus which was to become very welcome because it gave the Gollenese the luxury of very clean water with which to bathe, and very pure water to drink. It also had the advantage of dealing with the somewhat pungent smell which pervaded the atmosphere around most Gollenese, and surely would have a detrimental effect on the Tourist trade if not dealt with. The pure water was the result of the wonderful filtering it underwent as it found its way through the limestone rock of the high mountains to the north from which it sprang. There was an inexhaustible supply and a bottling plant lead to a second industry to Tourism. Mongollen water was soon to become a serious rival to Malvern Water, Highland Spring Water and many other such health drinks. Whilst the income from this would not match that of Tourism, the beauty of this second string was that 90% was agreed as the Gollenese share.

China felt that 10% was due to them as the works undertaken led to the discovery of the springs.

To revert to Task 2, filling from the springs could be commenced fairly easily from the north. From the south the upward slope presented a problem. In any event a new source of water was required, with the spring contribution likely not to be major in the short term. The solution lay with the Chinese again. Their oil industry had commissioned huge tankers from South Korea in the past, and it was not beyond them to adapt these to carry fresh water from abundant supplies on their territory south of Mongollen. The main problem of the elimination of all traces of crude oil was accomplished to complete satisfaction in their largest tanker and it was estimated that perhaps fifty trips to the emptying point would prove sufficient to give the lake a good start, and that over time the springs would finish the job. So far as this was concerned the problem of the upward slope in the south had to be overcome. Once again Prince Seamus came forward with an answer. In his University days he had stumbled into a lecture on the Archimedes Screw (as you will know this was the invention of Archimedes of Syracuse), and this was simply because Seamus was intrigued by the title. The memory of the Screw being used to propel liquids upwards against gravity remained with him, and surfaced on contemplation of the current problem. To his great credit he was able to bring this solution to a satisfactory conclusion so far as the Gollenese efforts were concerned and his Archimedes Screws were much admired. So much so in fact that an Institute of Science and Technology was commissioned by the King and Prince Seamus was appointed as the life President and given the title Professor of Fluid Mechanics. This put him on a par with the Professor at the Inner Mongolian University. Who, by the way, was not invited to put in his two yuan's worth as Seamus had intended earlier. It was a very nice touch to unearth the copy of Bernouilli's Equation which had resided in the Royal Palace to date. This was gilded in gold and silver and moved to the entrance to the Institute where it was installed in an elaborate glass case and retitled the Prince Seamus of Mongollen Equation. It remains the source of bewilderment it was originally and for that reason it is revered by all Gollenese. It was felt that the Presidency of the Institute was a fitting reward for Prince Seamus for his application of three scientific solutions to the PROBLEM and his familiarity with Bernoulli, Isaac Newton and Archimedes was much acknowledged.

The filling of Lake Titigollen to an acceptable level was finished by the Chinese who were able to pump empty their tanks from the piers on the coast up the main highway to the lake. This, of course was a far greater achievement than the local effort, but it must be remembered that the Chinese had the technical expertise and machinery necessary.

Fresh water fish of various kinds were introduced for the anglers expected, and Lake Titigollen became the idyll anticipated.

All in all the transformation of Mongollen was complete, including the training necessary to bring the Gollenese to the standard required as Hoteliers, Barkeepers, Restaurateurs, Waiters, Croupiers, Strippers, Pole dancers, Lap dancers, and the myriad other specialities required in the Tourist trade. These specialities the locals took to like ducks to water as well they might as it meant that the rather more prosaic agricultural work became much less attractive, and of course short in gratuities. Those in Tourism quickly learned Mandarin and English necessary in their trade, and this spread throughout the population. Agricultural production remained essential and a certain proportion of the labour force was detailed off to continue working on the land. This was reduced to a minimum by the introduction by Prince Seamus of modern methods of farming which this now earnest young man had studied since his elevation to a Professorship.

As of now Tourism is booming in Mongollen, the capital Cogollen has been modernised substantially, the Royal Palace enlarged and improved in all aspects. King Patrick, surprisingly, has by now created almost a replica of Buckingham Palace and incorporated into Palace life much of the ceremonial associated with the British Royal family. There is now a Guards Regiment, Blues and Royals on horseback, Changing of the Guard ceremonies, and even Garden Parties. All this has brought into being a class structure which is not to everyone's liking, particularly to the new lower class- mainly those in agricultural work, and in the more menial jobs in the Tourist trade. However it must be said that the GDP of Mongollen has increased exponentially and this has benefitted the populace as a whole to the extent that there are now no poor people.

King Patrick felt though there was something lacking and brought this to mind whilst reading about Prince Charles of the United Kingdom who he had come to admire greatly. He was intrigued to find that the Prince wished to be known as Defender of the Faiths. The title appealed to Patrick and wished it could be bestowed on him also. The rub of course was that there was no faith to be defended in Mongollen. So it was that religion was resurrected. There was a faint remembrance of Catholicism passed down through the generations of the more Irish, and of Buddhism, Shintoism and other Far Eastern religions in other of the Gollenese. King Patrick initiated a campaign to introduce the new Religion to the country, combining all felt to be good (as far as could be ascertained) in the different beliefs. However he instructed the MON GSS to keep a very watchful eye on any who became overzealous in their practice, which must not of course impinge in any way on the secularism in the country. Nor must different strands in beliefs lead to conflict which has been so evident in the world to date. At the first sign of deviation from these ground rules it would be met by total expungement of religion.

And so it was that the King became Defender of the Faiths, the title conferred upon him by the new Archbishop of Cogollen, an appointment made at the first meeting of the Synod. This was comprised of senior members of the Royal Family. Here they impressed the rest of the world by announcing Queen Queenie as the first female Archbishop. Anywhere.

This of course was an inspired choice as any fervour which might possibly be aroused by the common clergy could be stamped on from above, and in any event ordainment into the Priesthood would lay with the Synod guided by MONGSS. So the title of Defender of the Faiths could be interpreted rather differently from common usage.

Whilst initially the tourists were from the neighbouring countries of the Far East, it is now quite usual for visitors to hail from the West and from the U.S.A and Canada. And indeed some from Y Wladfa in Patagonia. Not, so far as it is known, that there is any wish there to emulate the changes made by Mongollen.

The Irish are coming in some numbers in view of the connection, and as a result there have been reciprocal visits by long removed kith and kin to the Emerald Isle. Some of the reverse tourists are a small number of Gollenese who saw a great deal of the new order as destructive of their old culture, and could not be persuaded that this must be a good thing. It is of course ironic that the very reasons Mongollen came into being so many years ago are now being reborn, but certainly there is not, to any appreciable amount, the wish or the will to return to the original template.

In any event visits to South West Ireland convinced a hard core of the disaffected that here was an ideal spot to move to, and it has reached the stage whereby agreement with the Irish may be possible and Boreland could well be established. The name was conjured up by O'Flaherty, leader of the movement known as the Brigade of Reluctant Educationees, known as Bores. In the new land the necessity for much of the modern paraphernalia would not be required, nor had it been in the old days. Whilst recognising that the history of Lake Titigollen had posed a problem which ultimately led to the new Mongollen, this was unlikely to pose the same problem on the coast of the wild Atlantic which was capable of eating the waste produced by the Bores for breakfast, in the words of the old homily.

The exit of O'Flaherty and his ilk will not affect Mongollen or its Resorts (Shangri Las Vegas and the Gollenese Riviera) to any great degree. They come from the lower classes, and King Patrick and family put their pique down to an absence of invitations to Garden Parties, and the total exclusion of their number to the receipt of New Year or Birthday Honours.

Ah well

As the Gollenese say:

C'est la vie

PART TWO

A word of warning:

Mongollen Part 2 contains a reference to Triad tattoos and their removal which may not be to the liking of some of the readership who I hope will be attracted by the Mongollen stories in general. In particular I am thinking of those of a genteel nature who might find the identification of a Triad member and the subsequent threat of removal of his tattoo a little too strong for their taste. Please overlook the passage and move to the happy ending if this is the case.

I am, of course, aware that by giving this warning I may be arousing the curiosity of those I am trying to protect, but in truth I am endeavouring to protect myself from criticism.

The Author

Having overseen the transformation of Mongollen to the present state, King Patrick and Queen Queenie made the decision that the time had come for them both to enjoy a pleasure filled retirement. Plans were made for a joint abdication in favour of their number one son Prince Seamus.

The King and Queen would spend their time between a new Villa to be built on the Gollenese Riviera and a separate wing in the Royal Palace in Cogollen. The Queen was to resign her Archbishopric, and revert to her normal religious status, which was perhaps not as zealous as might be imagined. A suitable replacement would be appointed by the Synod, and he, or she, was quite likely to be from the Family and as such probably of the same order of zeal as the first Archbishop.

None of this of course, was a fly in the ointment. Surprisingly this turned out to be Prince Seamus who was distinctly cool in his appraisal of his life as King.

He had altered from a rather swashbuckling, fun loving young Prince into a serious student of all Sciences and Arts, and against all predictions had proved capable of absorbing, and indeed excelling in both spheres. Earlier he had relied on a pensive visage to justify his Presidency of the College of Science and Technology, which now incorporated the Humanities and Arts. Prince Seamus now fitted the bill admirably and was instrumental in promoting a great surge in the desire of many Gollenese for higher education.

He was right to expect that ascendancy to the Throne would severely restrict the time he could devote to the work of the Institute and this he found unacceptable.

His desire for learning and dissemination of knowledge was widened to a passion with his introduction to Dr. Li Le Lo, a PhD of Gollenese descent, a star pupil through her Degrees, Masters and Doctorates in both Science and Arts. She began her academic career at Beijing University at a very young age, and it was quite apparent from the beginning that she was capable of absorbing knowledge like an endless supply of blotting paper receiving ink from an overflowing ink well.

Following her so successful University life she had the urge to return to her native Mongollen, and applied to the Institute of Science and Technology for a post designated as Vice Chancellor. She was interviewed by Prince Seamus who was overwhelmed.

Not only by her Academic profile. She was extremely pretty, in her mid 20's (slightly younger than the Prince) pretty in a way which was not to be expected after the rigorous learning curve she had undergone. Certainly many of us would feel it a little unfair that so much brain and beauty had been visited on one person. At the very least one would expect a furrowed brow, with eyes less bright and blue after acres of print had passed before them, and with a stoop brought on by constant hunching over an uncomfortable desk. Any discomfort one might feel on these scores not being realised would happily vanish when she was introduced because she was delightful in her social skills.

As we know Prince Seamus marvelled at all her charms. Li Le Lo (Lily as she was to be addressed later by Seamus) in her turn revealed that her interests were not restricted to Academia. She was struck with love at first sight when she presented herself for interview with Prince Seamus. And why not? She was a fully rounded woman with normal appetites for love, companionship and a sharing of congenial interests and Prince Seamus was an exceedingly handsome and virile young man.

In the first few weeks of Dr. Li Le Lo's appointment (could anyone doubt that the post was hers from the first minute of interview) she had expanded Prince Seamus's knowledge in all respects, and it was soon evident that they would marry. Lily was an O'Gollen as so many of the Gollenese are but this was no barrier to the union as any family connection was so obscure as to be discounted. Nor was there any disapproval from the King and Queen and the extended family, all of whom were so welcoming. She would become Princess Li Le Lo of Mongollen, and plans were put in hand for the wedding at Queens Cathedral (yes, one had been constructed earlier modelled on St. Paul's in London). The wedding was to be a la mode that of Princess Elizabeth and Prince Philip in 1947 which augured well for the longevity of the marriage to come.

The King and Queen were hopeful that the marriage would prove a spur to the Prince and Princess ascending the Thrones as King and Queen, leaving the present King and Queen as King Father and Queen Mother. Notwithstanding this Prince Seamus was adamant that his life henceforth was to be in education exclusively, and certainly his Princess in no way tried to influence his decision. This was viewed by most as commendable, realising that the temptation to advance to being a crowned head of a nation, with all the glory that it might bring was resisted by a complete regard for her future husband's wishes. It was not doubted that his mind might well be changed by Lily if she sought so to do but she was wise enough to know that this was not the basis on which to embark on their union. And indeed she felt that his decision was the right one for both of them because in their life work they were very much in one mind.

Prince Seamus was conscious that it may be selfish to deny the King and Queen their desire to lay down the undoubted burden of Heads of State which they had accepted and carried successfully for a long time. In his mind there was a solution which rested with his sister Anna, two years his senior and the first born of King Patrick and Queen Queenie. Mongollen had adopted the same Law of Succession as the United Kingdom, and on this basis she was ruled out as Queen in favour of Seamus who was to succeed. He approached Anna to confirm what he had always felt; this being that Princess Anna would prove to be a formidable Monarch, capable of propelling Mongollen to heights hitherto undreamed of. This was precisely the feeling that Anna had herself, but sisterly love had prevented her espousing her cause and she would support Seamus to the ultimate.

She was aware that the Law of Succession in the United Kingdom was changed in 2013, and Princes would no longer take precedence over their older sisters, bringing an end to the rule of male primogeniture which had been in place since the Act of Settlement in 1701, and was followed in Mongollen. This did not affect Princess Anne in the UK as she was second born, but it could affect the position in Mongollen where Princess Anna was the first born. Princess Anne made this point to Princess Anna who was a similar mould to her, and they had become good friends despite the 25 years or so between them. The friendship came about through contact with each other in various stages of Mongollen which echoed much of the British Heritage.

Prince Seamus respected his sister greatly, although always a little in awe of her. He was not alone in this and she was sometimes referred to as Princess Annaconda (but not in her hearing) having a propensity for man eating if called upon by any male (or indeed female) with ideas which she considered infantile and futile. In this respect she was like Princess Anne who was rather forthright in her views.

Anna took little convincing that she would be a good Queen, and it would not be long before her subjects agreed, although retaining warm feelings for Prince Seamus. The solution was put to King Patrick and Queen Queenie who approved the plan as sound provided the amendment to the Law of Succession could be passed, and incorporate retrospective action to date from the birth of Princess Anna. This did not pose a problem; you will recall that there was no opposition party to muddy the waters if they so felt, and the amendment was passed unanimously.

However there was some misgiving that the benign Monarchial style of King Patrick and Queen Queenie might become less benign under Queen Anna. She had the instinct to acknowledge this to herself, and was fully aware that she would require the full support of her people to take Mongollen forward. She did not adopt the hectoring approach expected, and sought help from her Parliament in the establishment of an Opposition bench, but not of course in opposition to Her Majesty. Whilst the British template was to be adopted in part, not to the degree of liberalism enjoyed there. Anna felt that Mongollen must learn to walk before galloping into the freedom of pure democracy, with every chance of being dismounted by the cruel joust of realism. There was to be a clear understanding that proposed legislation would be approved at the highest level (the Queen) before appearing on the Statute Book. Additionally, whilst a regular audience with the Queen was to be granted to the Prime Minister, yet to be confirmed, he would be left in no doubt that it may not be as pleasant as at Buckingham Palace, as Anna's thoughts on the business of the day would be expressed forcibly.

Having cleared the decks as it were, there followed the abdication of King Patrick and Queen Queenie, henceforth to be King Father and Queen Mother. By common acceptance the new Queen was crowned at Queens Cathedral, and shortly after, the wedding of Prince Seamus and Princess Li Le Lo was celebrated there. Both events were a great success, bringing with them two Bank holidays (a sure sign of progress in Mongollen since this story began).It also brought together more closely the mutual esteem between the two Royal families of Mongollen and the United Kingdom, the latter represented by Princess Anne and Prince Charles at both celebrations.

It is strange that Mongollen came into existence as the Irish founders sought to distance themselves from English Royalty and now emulated it in many ways. But that is the case.

To the extent that Queen Anna had by her side a potential Consort. His name was Liam Flynn – same surname as the old film star mentioned earlier but with no claim to relationship in spite of following the same career to an extent. He had established a decent reputation in action films but not to the same degree. Indeed his heart was not entirely in the silver screen or the stage.

Liam, now in his late 30's, arrived in Mongollen a year or so prior to the abdication and was so taken with the country that he filed for Gollenese citizenship. His pedigree was given as Irish and accepted by the vetting committee, and he was readily endorsed as a citizen.

He came to the notice of Princess Anna whilst playing Shylock in the Merchant of Venice. The stage and screen had been part of Liam's background, but not by any means his life's work. He lived in Southern Ireland on an estate which he managed for an absent landlord. Here he was concerned with organic farming, running of the estate with an interest in ecology. This is not to say he eschewed the lighter side of life.

Liam was an accomplished swimmer, surfer and dancer with a love of Irish culture and an ability on the fiddle which assured him of an invitation to all parties. He was also an exponent of the Irish Riverdance which he was to take to a new level by including in this the Hopak Ukrainian Cossack dance as part of a performance by a group of Gollenese dancers he was training. The athleticism required is of the highest order and promises to be a world beating dance. He felt that whilst his work on the estate, and his general lifestyle gave him much satisfaction, arriving in Mongollen may open up opportunities for an even more fulfilling life. He had little idea of his true potential, but hoped that a complete change would realise it fully (and from Ireland to Mongollen was quite a change). However the precedent evident in all he saw in Mongollen was one which led to his decision to take up Gollenese citizenship.

Strange that he should return to the stage, and this arose when he was asked to stand in for Peter Chou, a Mongollen Thespian of some repute who had to take a leave of absence when he had a heavy cold. As a measure of the man, Liam opted to underplay the part of Shylock so as not to undermine the reputation of Mongollen's leading actor. It was not difficult for Liam to achieve this as he was not a Shakespearian actor. He and Peter Chou became firm friends with very similar thoughts on the future of the Country in which they were to play significant roles.

Princess Anna was impressed and met Liam backstage and learned his story and of his aspirations. Although the impression of Princess Anna may have formed in the reader's mind as a young lady of autocratic and imperious mien, it should be acknowledged that, in common with most of the Royal family, she was extremely good looking and had a rather soft side. She could be very loveable, with a depth of feeling not always on display. This was evident to Liam from the first few meetings and whilst understanding the position of authority that she represented so diligently, he was conscious that she was a person who needed to cushion herself from the arduous nature of her future as Queen by a private life shared with a companion who could bring contentment and happiness with love.

Anna and Liam saw each other on a regular basis prior to her coronation and their feeling for each other deepened into true love. However Liam had understandable qualms about taking this to the normal conclusion and could not bring himself to accept that Queen Anna, as she now was, wished to have him by her side as Consort. Her advisors, mainly her family, realised that she would need the closest support from a staunch and loyal companion to carry forward her ambitions for the Country. In this regard they had come to feel that Liam Flynn was a man of honour and integrity who had the potential to fulfil the role of Prince Consort made his own by Prince Philip, Duke of Edinburgh. Certainly Liam had looked for a change in his life by moving to Mongollen, and slowly he came to the conclusion that as Consort to the woman he loved there was the opportunity to do rather more than appear as a celebrity of stage and screen, and he would readily admit that in this he could not aspire to the heights. Nor did he wish to; the image had palled some time ago.

The possibility of a Royal Wedding was a common talking point in the Capital and throughout the Country, and it was evident that the union would be well received. Liam Flynn had mixed freely with his (now) countrymen, and although there was an element of popularity brought about by the showing of his films the underlying acceptance was clear to see.

So, after soul searching and discussions with the Queen and her advisors, Anna and Liam were to be married and this, at Queens Cathedral was as wonderful an occasion as the two gone before. Another Bank holiday gratefully received by the masses.

And for the Queen and her Consort (now elevated to Prince Consort Liam) a honeymoon in London where the Prince received advice from the Master on the duties of Prince Consort. This was freely given by Prince Philip who advised him of all the traps to be avoided, a number of which he had not.

Princess Anne and Queen Anna cemented their friendship, and the British people took the couple to their hearts.

And so back home.

Again, all is well in Mongollen then ?

I am sorry to say that this was not the case.

There was a PROBLEM in Mongollen.

This centred on the Shangri Las Vegas resort and the generally hedonistic lifestyle which is a mainstay for the Tourist industry. It is hardly surprising that, in common with its counterpart in Las Vegas in the United States, it should attract those with an interest in a fast buck – or in this case with a fast yuan. This was perpetuated with a vicious gangsterism persuading victims to be fleeced by the imposition of protection money which was now demanded by one of the smaller Triad organisations called the Lei Triad who were the first of the very many Triads in China (and indeed elsewhere) to recognise the welcome source of income born on their borders. Having established this as their territory the others followed the unwritten rule of the Triads not to muscle in. There were many instances of inter Triad wars, but generally not for interference when the prey was clearly identified by one Triad exclusively. Honour among thieves.

Part of the resort's attractions had brought with them predictable additions, including a drug scene, prostitution and a general low life not welcome to most Gollenese including the Royal family and the Government. It was clearly on the agenda of Queen Anna to face this but the intention had not reached a stage to implement a strategy to deal with it. It was here that Princess Lily was able to put into the picture her knowledge of the Triad secret society groups, because she had made a comprehensive study of them at University, and her Thesis which led to a PhD was regarded as definitive on the subject. She was able to produce a report to convince the Queen and

Government that an offshoot of the Hong Kong Triads Wo Hop To was controlling completely the entertainment at Shangri Las Vegas. This was the Lei Triad and whereas Wo Hop To members numbered around 50000 their offshoot was in the hundreds of hardened criminals, independent of the main Triad, and acted without orders or input from Hong Kong. There Wo Hop To was encountering stiff opposition to its own operations and according to Princess Lily, unlikely to take an interest outside its own difficulties. There was increasing law enforcement in many parts of the world being brought to bear against organised crime and the Triads and Mafiosa were feeling it to their discomfort.

In Shangri Las Vegas the foothold of the Lei Triads was firmly was established when one casino was burned to the ground and its management brutally murdered for not agreeing to the 10% protection money traditionally expected. Following this every casino, restaurant, bordello etc. took on this overhead.

Princess Lily stressed that the Lei Triad, although small by most Triad standards, was able to muster several hundred members, headed by experienced leaders, well organised and led by a Dragon Head or Mountain Master, Vanguard being head of organisation, a Deputy Mountain Master, an Incense Master and Red Pole the enforcer and others. All well known titles in the Triad world and all with specific roles to play. She was very clear that Shangri Las Vegas faced a ruthless Crime syndicate and they must fight fire with fire.

As a result of the friendship between Prince Liam and Peter Chou, discussions took place at the highest level concerning the manner in which an offensive could be launched, and one of the first agreements was that

Parliament should be better organised and strengthened. To this end there should be an effective Prime Minister voted in by the people (but with the approval of the Queen who was not yet tuned into complete democracy). Peter Chou was approved by the Queen and as a well known Gollenese and popular as a stage performer, he was voted in overwhelmingly. His wife En Lai was elected as Leader of the Opposition. She loved her husband very much, but she, of all people, was fully aware of any shortcomings in his nature, and to her mind the greatest of these was that he could be rather too easy going in his dealings, and required occasionally to be harder in his decisions. As Leader of the Opposition she would be in a position to sharpen up his response to the difficulties which undoubtedly he would face, the biggest of which currently was to bring Parliament to one mind in the war against the Lei Triads which was to be declared.

His first move was to establish various Ministries to deal with Defence, Health, Treasury, Education, and the plethora of political posts necessary to govern, which previously had been on an Ad Hoc basis, according to what expertise was vaguely recognised in the corridors of power in Mongollen. Indeed most was the prerogative of King Patrick and Queen Queenie who accepted the burden with good grace, and with some success. However the situation was very much more complex than it was and Queen Anna, her Consort, the Prime Minister and the Leader of the Opposition recognised this. Peter Chou sharpened up rather surprisingly in his appointments to the Ministries (with the tacit approval of Mrs.Chou) which were made with regard to strength of character, and with no influence of personal friendship, but with absolute conviction that the choices were totally on merit. Peter Chou ignored many approaches by long standing friends for posts which he felt were beyond their range of abilities. In the event he selected a number who were likely to disagree with him on certain issues, but he regarded this as a healthy contribution to the overriding plan to ensure the best possible outcome to their mutual interest in a better Mongollen.

The regular audiences with the Queen was of great importance, for the conduit for relaying the feeling of the people had been lost when Liam was less able, for reasons of protocol, to mix freely with them. Prime Minister Chou filled that void admirably and the meetings with Queen Anna were not as daunting as he expected. Mainly because they were very much on the same wavelength, and, like Liam, the Queen had a high regard for him.

At this critical time the most urgent appointment was the choice of a Minister of Defence and War to lead the assault against the Triads. It was agreed without dissent that a forceful character named Joseph O'Gollen, with a pedigree going back to the early settlement of the Irish should take the reins. Joseph was a Gollenese of fierce patriotism and the man to fight fire with fire. His first step was to push through Parliament an Act to designate the Lei Triad a Proscribed organisation which was unlawful. This was to be the legal basis for any action by the Government however punitive. There was little doubt that Joseph O'Gollen would visit very severe punishment on anyone found to be a Triad member.

It was not surprising that he had little confidence in the existing Police Force or Secret Service being up to the task ahead. This was not a reflection of the will, but simply as a result of inexperience of the level of crime visited upon them. The Gollenese themselves were instinctively law abiding and provided little difficulty for the authorities in keeping the peace. In due time and with outside training, they would no doubt rise to a level to be able to counter any resurgence of gangster-ism, but as of now, Joseph O'Gollen required the resources to deal with the present serious situation.

Mongollen, you will recall had an Army. This was purely ceremonial and recruited for the Tourist trade; they performed beautifully whilst changing the Guard, and whilst Trooping their colour, albeit earned spuriously in the absence of any war experience. They figure on thousands of photographs alongside visitors to the country, and in splendid uniforms were truly most impressive.

This, by the way, would have been less impressive had King Patrick and Queen Queenie (mainly the Queen) not vetoed the original headgear suggested. This was based on the Bearskin or Busby worn by the Guards in Britain. The Gollenese were of a rather smaller stature and the Queen felt the volume involved in a furry abomination (her description) was no more than a slavish admiration for all things English, and would not sit well on a small head. The headdress approved was modelled on that worn by the Gurkha Regiment of Nepal who were more akin to the Gollenese size.

Joseph O'Gollen required a fighting force capable of empowering the Proscribing Act by expelling the Lei Triads from Mongollen. He anticipated that this would not easily be achieved, and he did not hesitate in promoting his view that any opposition should be dealt with in the most rigorous manner, including "taking out" if this was called upon as the ultimate sanction. "Taking out" is of course an euphemism for murder, or in this case legal execution. Joseph would not flinch from this authorisation, no more than the Triads do against opposition to their will.

So he had two problems to face. First the fighting force and second the identification of Triad members, who did not generally attract attention to themselves unless attending to their mundane business of reinforcing their hold over the Resorts by periodic beatings etc. when aware of small transgressions of their laws.

In general then they did not all stand out as Triads, some would be looked upon simply as visitors from Hong Kong, many were indistinguishable from the Gollenese, spoke the language and ran small businesses legitimately. But remained true to their oath of allegiance taken at initiation; had they demurred at any Triad action or participation when called upon the punishment was horrific.

Princess Li Le Lo believed she had the answer to the identification problem. Her researches had involved a study of all Triad organisations, large and small. Of the smaller syndicates the Lei Triad had greatly interested her. Most people are aware that the Tattoo business is supported considerably by the Triads and some were very impressive in their body art. Indeed this has now spread to all strata of society in the Western world and elsewhere – no celebrity is much rated in the absence of some painfully etched adornment to their legs, arms necks etc. A great pity, some will feel, for many are hideous blemishes on perfectly attractive bodies. Names will not be mentioned but I have no doubt some will spring to mind. A simple anchor on a seaman's biceps is no longer viewed as sufficient.

The Lei Triads stood alone in this world of Tattoos; they were not as heavily burdened as some with these adornments, but in one regard they were stoic in accepting pain by having the Triad triangle tattooed on a part of their body rarely exposed to anyone but themselves and their nearest and dearest. The imagination boggles but you are correct in the conclusion you have reached. By the way, this tattoo was restricted to the male member. Lady members were less discreetly marked out as they were hardly an important part of the organisation. This was not dwelled on in the information which Princess Lily imparted to Joseph O'Gollen and his committee.

The difficulty was to reach a point where a suspected Triad member could be persuaded to expose himself. Some outlandish suggestions were made by the more worldly members, but were discounted because a Triad was not of the persuasion that would lead to a voluntary exposure, particularly when the request would be viewed as coming from a pervert.

There was no doubt in the mind of the Minister of Defence and War that the only possible way to identify a Triad was by brute force, followed by a stark choice of immediate expulsion from Mongollen with no worse than injured pride, or mutilation of the member in removing the offending Tattoo.

To arrive at that happy solution was hardly within the competence of the existing Law Enforcement Agents, but through involvement of Queen Anna it could be brought about.

Princess Anne was due to pay a visit to Nepal, where she had the interests of the Gurkha Regiment in the service of the British Crown, and the family members at home in Nepal very much to heart.The Gurkhas were renowned for their fighting qualities, and in extending her visit to include Mongollen Princess Anne felt that there may be an opportunity to provide assistance in stiffening Mongollen's Forces to a degree that might give them a chance of meeting the Triad threat. This would be by involving the Gurkhas to train up the existing Army. This recommended itself to the Gurkha Regiment who would be granted leave of absence from their duties on behalf of the British Army, which Princess Anne felt she would be able to engineer.

Queen Anna was much taken by the plan put forward by her good friend, and she lost no time in seeking out the approval of the Minister and his Committee.

In the meantime though Joseph O'Gollen had reason to explore an avenue which he felt could be effective, particularly if it could be linked to the Queen's proposal.

Generally the Gollenese were a peaceable lot and this extended to the Gollenese Army unfortunately. However there was a strain of Gollenese in the northern hills and mountains of the country who endured the harsher conditions in that part of Mongollen, and this had imbued in them a hardiness completely lacking in the south. The main living centred on an equally hardy breed of goat in Gurgollen, which name came about by the distant relationship with the Nepalese, although first and foremost the northerners were patriotic Gollenese.

The goatherds were a source of a good income, being the producers of remarkable cheeses sought after world wide, and the Gurgollens had perpetuated this excellence over a long period by judicious neutering of rams judged to be not up to the standard set. Joseph had been present to witness the operation first hand and had been fascinated by the expertise shown in the ease of handling the kukri type knife used by the Gurgollen men. To the degree that he pictured this in the removal of the Triad Triangle tattoo. This gave him great pleasure and a burning ambition to incorporate the Gurgollens in the fight to rid the country of the Lei Triads.

He did not hesitate to ask for the help of the northeners in combatting the evil in the resorts, and was surprised to find that little was known by them concerning this. In fact they had only a vague picture of the new Mongollen nor did they seek to explore it with any enthusiasm. Notwithstanding this, they had a high regard for the Royal family, had marvelled at the time when Prince Seamus produced his Equation, revered the Kings and Queens from the first, and would serve them in any way required.

When appraised of this by the Minister, Queen Anna and Prime Minister Chou visited the Gurgollens to express their grateful thanks for their loyalty. This was well received, as was the intention to bring in a number of Nepal's finest soldiers to train the new Force up. These were perfectly willing to take a more active part in the mayhem to be visited on the Triads. In the event this was little called upon, for after initial training in military discipline, the Gurgollens adopted their own methods of warfare, which proved to be fierce and unforgiving.

As it happened this was to the advantage of the ceremonial Army, and it became the Gurkhas task to bring them up to speed as a realistic fighting force. This may seem to be an unlikely outcome, but as things stood there was a transformation in the attitude of the Army, and a wish to be divested of the chocolate soldier image, and to be recognised as real soldiers capable of meeting any future threat. The Police Force and Intelligence service followed in the wake of the Army, and brought in outside expertise to up their game.

The initial training of the Gurgollens impressed the Gurkhas, who were disappointed to conclude that their own contribution to the forthcoming crusade was likely to be minimal, such was the dedication to castration exhibited by the new recruits.

However, looking to the future, this was probably all to the good, as it hastened the training of the Gollenese Army to be a realistic fighting force which could fulfil a role in the future, and in the short term be useful in the mopping up stage of the struggle shortly to begin.

The first step to combat was for the Defence and War Ministry to introduce the Gurgollens to the resort pleasure centres as Doorkeepers, Bouncers and Security staff. This was not objected to by the Lei Triad leadership who were pleased to view this as collaboration by the Gollenese. It was gratifying to be relieved of the tedious employment on the doors which largely was uneventful.

The number required was not huge, and those chosen by Joseph O'Gollen were armed with the precise wording of the Act proscribing the Triad syndicate unlawful. Also of course with the kukri knife. The first was of course to comply with the law before commencing the enforcement which was looked forward to by the northeners with glee. Behind those in place as the spearhead, the main body to be called on were similarily briefed on the Act.

At this stage the happy prospect of engaging in the enterprise was heightened by the somewhat narrow minded view of Shangri Las Vegas which had been formed by the Gurgollens' short acquaintance with the lifestyle. This of course was very much at variance with their own, and was regarded as somewhat sinful. It was stressed by the Minister, whilst accepting their views as perfectly understandable considering the Gurgollens severe and strict upbringing, it was essential that solid proof of Triad membership should be established before the choice of expulsion from the country or mutilation to remove the proof was undertaken.

In the beginning of course the choice was not given; strategy demanded early warning that quarter could not be expected if the end result (not a pun) was to be achieved. This is entirely in keeping with the view that Joseph O'Gollen would be fierce in his approach. Whilst official approval was not given to the exemption of choice allowed to the first suspects, tacit approval was implicit in ignoring protests by the victims.

The Minister though was conscious that he must toe a line to avoid any reduction in Tourism as a result of mistaken indentification. The solution he came up with was to confirm suspects cleared by a letter "C" to be imprinted on the forehead. This was to be in treated goat's blood which was reasonably long lasting, not easily erased and in the absence of a supply available to the Triads could not be used by them as a ploy to avoid challenge.

Those Gollenese cleared, and some Tourists it must be said, bore the "C" as a mark of honour. Indeed those visitors returning home were able to introduce an exciting talking point which lasted a month or so before fading under the onslaught of soap and water. Many spared the soap and water to extend their fame a few days.

Provided the struggle by passed the Tourists it turned out that the excitement gave an extra boost to the Industry. To witness a challenge by Gurgollens to Triad suspects was to participate in an adventure not to be found in any other package tour. The initial serious de bagging was entertaining; the identification hilarious, but the third stage in which the kukri figured was not for the squeamish. To witness the whole procedure was the boast of relatively few Tourists and reference did not appear in any of the Tour operatives'brochures. Those challenged and bore the "C" mark were forever grateful for passing the Test, possibly with a slight feeling of humiliation experienced in the process which lingered.

It was not the intention that the Gollenese/ Triad War should become a spectator sport which seemed to be the way it was heading and so it was that the Minister requested the Gurgollens to keep it out of the public domain so far as possible. This was accepted by them, for certainly they were not of a type to indulge in showmanship, and generally operated without an audience, happy indeed to do so for they felt it undignified to be applauded for a skill in debagging etc.

The Triads of course were not without courage or spirit, and fought back as well as they could, but in the face of such sustained ferocity, and reinforced with a huge resource in the Gurkhas in reserve, they came to the conclusion that they were fighting a losing battle.

More and more the Triads opted for voluntary expulsion under the Proscription as an unlawful organisation; those who had resisted were wheel chaired over the border by their companions, and left with their tails between their legs. Or in their case without.

The whole campaign took a short time only; it was hardly mentioned in Triad history and the Lei Triad was dissolved, never to reappear. In Mongollen Joseph O'Gollen was honoured by Queen Anna in a well attended ceremony at the Palace where a State Banquet was held at which the leadership of the Gurgollens were present. The unelected but widely accepted head of the northern forces was a Michael Rourke admired greatly by the Minister for Defence and War who offered him a post in the Ministry. Michael declined the offer for he was missing his goats terribly, and in any event did not wish to involve himself too deeply in the somewhat shallow (to his mind) way of life so much in contrast to his upbringing. Joseph and Michael remained staunch friends and visits by Prince Seamus and Princess Lily to Gurgollen led the way to closer ties between the two provinces in the Kingdom. In the course of much increased exchange visits it became apparent that whilst in the view of the southerners Gurgolleneses lived a less joyful life than themselves, this was not entirely true. This had been the view before much was seen by visitors, but increasingly they were present at Gurgollen pastimes which centred on dancing of the energetic Russian type, of singing male voice and mixed choral music somehow descended from a Welsh tradition. This suggested the original Gollenese had been infiltrated by emigrants at first destined for Patagonia, but who had boarded the wrong ship.

Wrestling of the pure Greco Roman tradition was also to the forefront as was horsemanship on the hardy mountain ponies, and in all there was generally an unlimited supply of goats mares milk wine (akin to the staple drink of the original Gollenese known as airag and in Gurgollen became Gairag). You may recall from earlier in the story that airag was not fiercely alcoholic by itself, but very stiff when mixed with porter. Gairag was inherently more alcoholic on its own and when taken with goats black pudding as an accompaniment could lead to very high spirits indeed. It is readily seen that the gap between the north and south was narrowed as a result of the increasing friendship.

On one of his visits The Minister for Defence and War took it upon himself to get involved in Church Synod business as he became aware that the vacated position of Archbishop had still to be filled. This he felt could be filled by Michael Rourke's father, much admired in the north for his unremitting devotion to his religion. News of this filtered through to the Synod and the members were appalled at the thought that zeal of the highest order would be introduced. Fortunately Rourke senior was equally disenchanted with the idea, fearing his corruption by the wayward ways down south. He declined the suggestion, and the Synod acted swiftly to appoint a more congenial Archbishop, their current Chairman, the Very Reverend Mcintyre Tung. Those of the Royal Family approached suggested that they were perhaps less zealous than Mcintyre Tung. Marginally so but it was felt better to exclude the Family at this time.

Drawing to a close it should be said that a slightly contentious issue reared its head. The Confederation of

Entertainment Business opposed the Prime Minister, the Treasury and the Government as a whole in their intention to alter the Taxation Laws by passing an additional tax on their enterprises. This proposed that the "protection insurance" of 10% paid to the Triads should be converted into an additional impost to fund national needs for a better Health service, for better Education and for Age Care homes. This was to be in addition to tax already levied but as it did not reduce the bottom line of the recent profit and loss accounts of the businesses identified, there was no real argument left to the C E B. Certainly it was felt by most that no way should they benefit from the triumph over the Triads other than by freedom from fear.

The Act was passed without opposition in Parliament and the Country settled to an improving standard all round; the Royal family were as popular as ever, Queen Anna was recognised as a worthy Sovereign and her husband as a Consort of the mould of Prince Philip, the Duke of Edinburgh, to be trusted and admired as the Queen's right hand. Prime Minister Chou continued as a first class Leader of his Party, the Opposition was forthright in its views where they differed from the Government, and Prime Minister's Question Time was a lesson to the British Parliament in its civilised behaviour. It was conducted in a pleasant manner engendered by the Prime Minister's address to the Leader of the Opposition as "my Honourable Wife" and responded by En Lai referring to "my Honourable husband".

Prince Seamus and Princess Lily promoted higher education as the way forward for the country, the Father King and Mother Queen prospered in their retirement and were likely to live to a ripe old age on the Gollenese Riviera where they increasingly spent their time, but always available for State functions and to stand in for Royal duties if required.

All is well then in Mongollen?
Yes it is.
C'est la vie.
As the Gollenese would say.

Postscript

It may be as well for future reference, if events in Mongollen prove worthy of recording, to have a fuller picture of the Royal family beyond Patrick and Queenie, Queen Anna and Prince Seamus.

King Patrick and Queen Queenie had three children junior to Anna and Seamus.

They were Prince Rory- a happy choice of name for he became a devoted fan of Rory Mcilroy. He was of course well known in Mongollen for his golfing architecture, and under tutelage by him Prince Rory became a scratch golfer well known on the amateur scene throughout the world. Beyond this he earned additional stripes as the founder of the Mongollen Air Force, small but enthusiastic flyers who were led by the Prince, a pilot of exceptional talent and daring.

To his credit also he was the leading proponent in the idea that the original airport built as part of the infrastructure by the Chinese should be enlarged to deal with the increasing Tourist trade, and Mongollen will shortly have the facilities to deal with the largest jets. He is, I believe, to be consulted by Boris Johnson on the London options.

His two sisters Molly and Trudy, twins of striking beauty were much in demand for all Royal festivities. There was great interest in them from all sides, and they were courted by world celebrities which, it must be said, left them open to seductive flirtations to scandalise at times. This, of course, provided a welcome diversion from the more mundane lives of the masses. Essential in some ways to maintain the deep interest in the Monarchy although not always appreciated by Queen Anna and mother and father. Notwithstanding, the Queen was first to welcome their willingness to take on Royal duties whenever asked; they performed extremely well as Openers of many buildings, as Patrons of innumerable Charities, and (their favourite role) as Joint Colonels in Chief of the Blues and Royals.

You will be happy to read that the Queen and Prince Liam were by now expecting their first child, who, boy or girl would be first in line for the throne. The future for Mongollen looks bright.

PART THREE

To continue with the saga it may be helpful if the Royal family was more clearly made known. But, being so numerous, perhaps not to more than the main players in the story to come.

So we have King Patrick and Queen Queenie, with two brothers of Patrick, and two sisters of Queenie:

Michael (58)	Josephine (55)
3 sons of Irish extraction	married to Connor-2 sons
Padraig (57) - two daughters Mixed Irish/Gollenese extraction	Mary (50) –married to Brendan
	No children

Patrick and Queenie, as we know, with daughter Anna, sons Seamus and Rory, and younger twin daughters Trudy and Molly. Queen Anna now married to Prince Liam and with their first baby boy named Patrick. Seamus with Princess Li Le Lo awaiting their first child.

You may recall that at the time of the abdication of King Patrick and his Queen the natural succession was thwarted by the disinclination of Seamus to take up the reins of Monarchy for worthy reasons.

To his Uncle Michael the outcome was judged to be a step too far by which the throne was usurped, and the method by which this was achieved was underhand to ensure that Patrick's children were not to be denied a continuation of his line. This was a result of the retrospective change to the Law of Succession after which Queen Anna was crowned.

Patrick, at the time was aware of a certain coolness on the part of his brother, but to his credit did not attribute this to more than disappointment in the decision of Seamus to put his own future wishes first, and the King's acceptance of this without a more robust opposition.

In fact Michael fully expected that in the absence of another natural male heir other than Rory, who was certainly not likely to agree the elevation as his interest was bound up in aviation and a Mongollen Royal Air Force, to be approached as the only credible successor.

The unjust(to his mind) blindness of the rest of the Royal family to this as a solution to the difficulty without manipulation of the Law of Succession, was in his view quite wrong. It bred in him resentfulness, which when allied to a natural aggressive nature was to lead to trouble in the future.

So Mongollen has a PROBLEM.

A problem that could be bigger than the two which have gone before.

Unlike Patrick, who was rather easy going- laid back may be a better description – Michael was assertive and a typical inheritor of the Irish traveller traits which in the past led to a predominance in bare knuckle boxing. In Michael's case a hobby but also a money spinner. He was a professional fighter in his youth, his sons followed him and fought over the Far East and beyond to some effect. Michael, in his later days became over fond of the black porter which led to his retirement, but his love of boxing took him on to training and promotion in the professional ring. This was with considerable success and he became significantly wealthy and was able to establish a first class training camp in Gurgollen where the environment was sufficiently rigorous to test the fitness of his protegees. Road running over difficult terrain, fitness building in the gym, celibacy and an absence of black porter and garaig (apart from Michael's needs of course) was the happy lot of his string of fighters. His sons took to the regime with relish; they were the only likely heavyweights until the import later of some from Boreland, proposed by the defector O'Flaherty who gave up on Mongollen as it became more civilised and moved out to southern Ireland to establish a province more suited to his rougher tastes. Other than at the higher weight categories those Gollenese or Irish/Gollenese boxers dominated the lighter divisions and were able to compete with bantam, feather, light and middle in countries famous for champions at these levels such as Mexico, UK, Phillipines etc.

Padraig was a very different character. Not a wimp but certainly not aggressive. From an early age he had embraced Academia, as in his later years had his nephew Seamus; in fact Padraig was more celebrated than Seamus as the author of many Scientific, Historical and factual treatises, and indeed on the short list for the Booker Prize for fiction. He was much admired by Seamus and Princess Le Li Lo and a great deal of their time was spent together toning their little grey cells until they were the pinnacle of the intellectual peak in Mongollen and beyond. Padraig's two daughters seemed likely to follow in his footsteps; it would be strange if they did not, enveloped as they were from an early age in the esoteric world of father and mother- who by the way was a Gollenese lady of great learning, and Padraig's natural companion for life.

As to Mary, the younger of the daughters of the Father King and Queen Mother, she was married to Brendan; both were devoted Catholics, to the degree that Mary was overlooked by the Family when choosing a replacement Archbishop following the resignation of Queen Queenie from this Office. She was considerably higher on the scale of zealotry than the Rev. Mcintyre Tung who was chosen. You may recall that the feeling was that the Archbishop should not be too religious as few would be likely to follow a strict interpretation of the Ministry, and was sure to be a source of strife between those who did and who followed the path of righteousness by different routes, so familiar in the outcomes in friction in the religions of the world. Here you have a measure of the wisdom of King Patrick and Queen Queenie.

Mary harboured some resentment but lived her life for her religion. Brendan accepted this and was proud of her, but felt somewhat cheated by her attractive appearance which mirrored the happy tradition of Royal beauty in the O'Gollens. He realised quickly after marriage that Mary was born for a Nunnery and was disappointed in the lack of physical communion which to him in his courtship promised much in his imagination, which was given free rein. Beyond this very little but Brendan accepted this as a sign of real virtue.

In time he fell into celibacy and was a likely candidate for the Priesthood when married men were admitted.

What is it with these O'Gollens?

We see such disparity between the nature of brothers, siblings etc which underlines variety as the spice of life.

Mary and her elder sister Josephine were entirely different. Josephine was a lover of life on earth, lived it to the full, spread light and joy to the extent that Mary and Brendan felt excessive most of the time, and on occasion in Josephine's more abandoned moments, were horrified. Her husband Connor was built in the same delightful way, and they were followed by two sons who could not but grow into the same order of human beings, provided that the O'Gollen curse of disparity was not visited on them.

It is unlikely that the boys would follow their Aunt's lead to Sainthood, but this is a thought which cannot be discounted given examples the Family can point to over time. We will not go down this road here.

To be fair to Mary and Brendan, a great deal of their time was spent in prayer for the salvation of the souls of Josephine and Connor, and to shine a poorer light on these two sinners, they felt that the intercession of their betters lessened the need for them to plead and pray for themselves. Having said this please keep your regard for Josephine and Connor high, for as you know these are the people who make life worth living. You will recognise that they do not represent other than a natural joy which can light up our own world and prove an antidote to gloom and despondency.

Talking of gloom and despondency, we now come to Michael O'Flaherty, and closely linked with him we arrive at the PROBLEM.

He was upset at the path the Kingdom of Patrick was taking, being much enthralled by the example of the British Royal family, absolutely against the instincts of Michael, and the advancement into the modern world brought about by the solution to an earlier PROBLEM. Michael O'Flaherty and a goodly number of his tribe and followers of a similar persuasion, who had been content to carry on in the old fashioned way, migrated to the south of Ireland establishing a new conclave in a land to be known as Boreland (from their title of Brigade of the Reluctant Educationees) and settled well into the life they lived before, with a delightful freedom from flush toilets, regular bathing, education and all the fetters of a civilisation which was anathema to them. They retained a liking for black beer, and also a respect for the bare knuckle fighting at which they were extremely proficient.

Their settlement was fairly remote, and whilst the Irish Government had sanctioned the entry into their country – for after all the Borees were returning Irishmen and women- it cannot be said that the newcomers were entirely welcome.

First it must be said that the Southern Ireland we all know and love, the beauty of the country, the charm of the Irish, the lively entertainment to be enjoyed is absolutely at variance with what the Borees would introduce.This was quickly realised by immediate neighbours with some dismay. Moreover the newcomers were ready recruits for the I.R.A. which most hoped would disband in the light of the Peace process which had every chance of success in the south and in the northern six counties. O'Flaherty was not slow to join the extreme Provisionals, and rose to become fearsome in his hatred for the British. He took with him most of his followers, but less and less was the call to any sort of action which they hoped for. In fact they became an embarrassment to the leaders of the Separatists who were seeking a political solution to the Irish question in the north.

In earlier days Michael O'Flaherty and Michael O'Gollen were known to each other. Not as bosom pals, but as opponents in the Ring. Both were skilful and ferocious, they headed the heavyweight division in Mongollen and fought each other twice, both bouts won by Michael O'Gollen, but only narrowly. They had a mutual respect for each other which was cemented to a degree by O'Gollen's indifference to his brother's fascination with the British Royals and their way of life which Patrick and Queenie emulated a great deal of the time.

Michael O'Flaherty was not a persona non grata in Mongollen, he visited on occasion and became a closer acquaintance of Michael O'Gollen, when he introduced his two sons to the training camp in Gurgollen, where they became heavyweight fighters in the top echelon. Also introduced were a number of Boree fighters at lower weights and all were taken under the wing of the Royal trainer and promoter. O'Flaherty became a successful trainer himself and the new informal partnership prospered.

His visits to Mongollen were largely spent at Gurgollen, which did not carry the taint of the effete south, and he was able to tolerate the lifestyle there despite the obvious regard the Gurgollens had for the Royal family which he put down to stupidity. We know well that Gurgollens are not stupid, and in time he would be educated to that fact.

He moved back to Boreland from time to time, passed through Cogollen on his travels and saw at first hand the development of Mongollen to the civilised country it had become. Strange to relate that a reversion to the very old order was his greatest wish.

He had come to the conclusion that his propensity for trouble making at home was not welcome beyond the ranks of the Provisionals, and he had decided that he would disturb the equilibrium on the other side of the world, feeling that Mongollen was ready for a shake up of the new order.

Not a likeable man you will have labelled Michael O'Flaherty, a man with a gigantic chip in his shoulder, but by sheer force of will capable of carrying with him a number of followers. He supplied them with the chips necessary to imbue the wrong spirit, and hammered them home to shoulders in number. This was a great joy to him, and maybe we should allow him some pleasure in a joyless life.

As to his view of Mongollen he felt that a system working well, as it was, should be prodded, poked and stirred until it lost appeal. It could then be substituted for a system which was of less appeal save to those O'Flaherty afficiandos. The reasons behind this way of thinking cannot be fathomed beyond the basic love of anarchy for anarchy sake.

On his visits to Gurgollen, which became increasingly more frequent, O'Flaherty was thrown into the company of Michael O'Gollen and a quiet drink from time to time became a habit. They were joined by many of the O'Flaherty and O'Gollen fighters and supporters and at one of these occasions, when the brown beer flowed freely, O'Flaherty was able to tease out of the King Father's brother his version of the events following the abdication of the King and Queen, and his resentment at the outcome which had denied him the Throne. He stressed that nothing but patriotism and the wish to further the progress of Mongollen were the motives he felt.

Michael O'Flaherty was outwardly sympathetic and the germ of an idea was born and became the PROBLEM which Mongollen was now to be faced with.

It hinged on the unlikely alliance of the good (in Michael O'Gollen) and the bad (need we name him?)

It was put to Michael (now the Duke of Gurgollen, bestowed upon him as a sop in his view) that he would never take the lead as King, which he found a self evident conclusion, but that it was a shame that Mongollen was missing out on his great leadership qualities. He demurred somewhat at this, because he had a high regard for his niece Queen Anna, and to date he felt that she had performed as well as anyone could, particularly in the fight against the Triads, and in the manner in which she was bringing to the people the birth of a democracy. He did disagree with the close connection with the British Royals, and felt that this should be more distant, for unlike his brother and family he retained the memory of why Mongollen was settled by his forefathers. In this, of course he shared common ground with O'Flaherty, although certainly not to the vehement expressions of hatred which he seemed to express regularly.

O'Flaherty made the suggestion on a few occasions that in view of the manner in which the Monarchy had been perpetuated by the Royal family, against what he considered to be the normal constitutional procedure (that of moving to the only male Royal personage willing to take on the responsibility) then there was reason to move the country forward as a Republic. The idea was preposterous in the view of the Duke of Gurgollen but in due course he thought he saw some merit in the idea.

It was stressed by his main Republican sponsor that as President the Duke would be the worthy leader of his country, with undoubted talents of leadership, and the popularity to override the opposition to such a change-over which was likely to be stiff.

The Duke recognised this, and he himself had sympathy with such a view because his niece, her Consort and her Government were doing a good job in the administration of the nation's affairs. He had great respect for Queen Anna and in the circumstances was realistic enough to doubt that a Republican movement would be of sufficient strength to bring about a democratic change. A coup d'etat to abolish the Monarchy was anathema to him and there was no possibility that he would be part of such an event.

It is of no surprise that O'Flaherty was intent on a different approach. Unbeknown to the Duke he had recruited from his followers – mainly imported from Boreland – the makings of a Mongollen Republican Army. Their tactics were to follow the I.R.A template, and in a short time had made themselves known in the country by introducing terror bombings.

In response David Chou fell back on Joseph O'Gollen, Minister of Defence who had triumphed over the Triads. The opposition strength surprised the Republican Army and the conflict grew into targeted murder by the MRA and to bombings without warning. The distress caused to the Duke at this turn of events was shattering and it was evident to him that his unholy alliance was the cause of this unspeakable outcome in his country.

His brother Padraig comforted him as best as he could and became important in the Government fight against the MRA. He organised an Intelligence Unit which by good direction was able to anticipate much of the MRA's targets.

It was through his operatives - mainly Michael O'Rourke of Gurgollen – that the chief thrust of the MRA was discovered. O'Rourke had satisfied Michael O'Flaherty that in him he had a simple soul, easily swayed. In reality, as we know, he was a firm supporter of the Royal family, and the last man to contemplate any harm to them.

This was O'Flaherty's ultimate weapon after a less than conclusive result to all that had gone before. His reasoning was that only by the elimination of one of the much loved Royal family could the capitulation of the Government be expected. The Duke was ruled out as an incoming President, held in house arrest by the MRA and the obvious replacement was to be O'Flaherty himself.

He decided that the Father King Patrick was to be the sacrifice. The plan was to be based on the Brighton bombing by the IRA earlier. This was likely to be at his Riviera residence where it was felt security was least tight. He overlooked the result in that it did not bring the Thatcher Government to its knees. In fact it united the nation.

In his role as Chief of Intelligence, Padraig learned of the plot from O'Rourke, and had all the necessary mechanics to counter it. He communicated this to his brother and was astonished to learn, that in his view Patrick agreed with O'Flaherty that this would be a defining moment in the campaign. Above all else he felt that the conflict must be ended and in this sequence of events, all before would be judged immaterial whereas this would be abhorrent to his subjects who would react in such fury that the MRA would be obliterated in the nation's history. O'Flaherty was likely to suffer a painful death – at the hand of Michael O'Rourke, for justice sake.

The rest of the family, including the Queen Mother, were not to be told of Patrick's view that mere knowledge of the plot would not be sufficient. It had to reach its conclusion. It is hard to understand why the two brothers could allow this, but here The Father King revealed his will of iron which had generally been cloaked in his avuncular manner. He made his two brothers swear to secrecy.

And so it came to the finale for the Father King. It was also the finale for the Queen Mother. In the nature of loving wives Queenie was aware that something was going on in the life of her wonderful husband.For some time he had been unwell and she had nursed him to the extent that she had supervised his bathing, and she was surprised to find that he professed to be more able to handle this aspect of his life than recently. In discussing this with her brother in law Michael, now fully restored to the family love, he told her of the plot in the hope that Queenie would prove to be the one to change his mind. In a short time she recognised that the heroic answer to the Mongollen PROBLEM was to be faced.

The appointed day dawned, pinpointed by Padraig who did not impede the planting of the bomb under the bath by two disaffected plumbers attending a so called leak.

Patrick moved to the bathroom, as did Queenie who allowed no protestation save that she told

Patrick she knew all, and her one desire was not to live without him.

The result proved Patrick right to a staggering degree. O'Flaherty and his MRA were sought out in an outpouring of love for the past King and Queen; to the fore were the Gurgollens whose revenge took a familiar form. O'Flaherty was not heard of again, but it was known that he never reached Boreland. This was not mourned in Southern Ireland.

There are few words that can express the feelings of the Mongollen people when they learned the true facts of the supreme sacrifice of their late King and Queen. Their memorials are revered, standing proudly in the Cogollen cathedral. Their statues stand equally as proudly in the Mongollen Parliament. And every year there is a celebration of their lives which assures the continuation of the Royal line for many years to come.

The tragic figure of this history is, of course the Duke of Gurgollen, whose life now would be a constant reminder of his wounded pride. His family supported his renewal, honoured his resistance to all O'Flaherty's plans when the true nature was exposed, and he found solace in work which he could carry out quietly towards best governance as an unheard of advisor.

All is well in Mongollen again, but at such terrible cost.

C'est la vrai as the Gollenese would say.

CLOUD NINE

The more obituaries I read, the more conscious I am of the hidden depths of goodness most of us do not exhibit as generously as we should whilst we are here. I read of the recently departed as icons of sainthood not recognized fully in their lifetimes, and whilst the ultimate arbiter of sanctity is of course, GOD, I feel it quite possible that the outpourings of His flock below may influence His markings to a degree. Whilst omniscient, He retains a spark of humanity after all. On presenting themselves at the Pearly Gates hopefuls may well be met by Him in an avuncular rather than a critical mood. 5 out of 10 marks may well be uplifted a point or two on the ground swell of opinion below, despite lapses recorded by His stewards at the time. These incidentally are, in the main, Jesus and the various Disciples, with-a sprinkling of Popes, Archbishops and various Saints who have been awarded true Sanctity in their death time. It is surprising to find Judas is in the number of stewards despite a rather serious lapse on his part. It demonstrates God's capacity for forgiveness but I would not be surprised if Jesus feels a bit miffed. He cannot express this of course, particularly when he is so remembered for turning the other cheek.

Whilst I applaud the appointment of Judas, I have made a mental note not to avail myself of his services if it can be avoided.

Here of course I am presupposing that I am going to be admitted, and furthermore that I shall attract a favourable mark. It cannot however be ruled out that the abject failures so many of us have been prone to means that a marking of between 2 and five cannot be uplifted sufficiently to bring some hopefuls to near the ultimate bliss of CLOUD 9.

I have a feeling that accommodation in Heaven is measured by the supremacy of one cloud over others. CLOUD 9 has generally been thought of on earth as the ultimate in delight. In Heaven it is the benchmark by which other clouds are judged.

Those deemed worthy will be so happy and whilst nothing is settled I am given to understand that I have been granted a reservation extending to 3 months in limbo. I cannot recall which steward gave me this news, but I am fairly sure it was not Judas.

During the reservation period I am required to sharpen up my act so far as atonement is concerned and thus far I am not sure of the extent of my sins, or the order of seriousness in which they are viewed. Nor, quite honestly, have I much confidence in arriving at the right solution to atone.

I shall give this serious thought, but in the meantime I have permission to familiarise myself with Heaven. In this regard I have accepted the help of one of the lesser known stewards whose name escapes me at the moment, but who I shall refer to as Nick. He assures me that his father is not Old Nick.

The accommodation on Cloud Nine (I do not feel I shall be interested in a lesser cloud) is very comfortable without being pretentious.

It consists of two bedrooms (one of which I would use as a study) bathroom, wet room (en suite naturally) a very pleasant living room, small but fully fitted kitchen. Toilets are incorporated in the bathroom and wet room, but I am not sufficiently briefed at this time to know whether these will be necessary. Nor do I know whether a kitchen is necessary, but as these items are standard I must assume that this is the case.

Cloud Nine has a wonderful situation, giving as it does memorable and beautiful vistas of this Heaven, of other Heavens. Of an Earth bathed in perpetual sunshine, of stars and moons and all things bright and beautiful. The Lord God made them all. There is a hymn in the making there.

Neighbours on CLOUD NINE are generally of the same level of sanctity as each other and so occupiers are more or less guaranteed a peaceful and amicable existence. They tend not to stray downwards to lower clouds. This worries me a little as it smacks of elitism which is not a hallmark of sanctity.

CLOUD NINE is not the ultimate in Heaven, however judged on earth. There are a smaller number of Pent Houses on CLOUD TEN and above. They seem to be occupied by a number of senior clergy, saints etc. I was made aware by Nick of one Pope on Cloud 5. As to other Senior Clergy quite a few have been relegated to lower Clouds. Nick tells me there are no Politicians on clouds above 9, and few of them at this level. As you would expect standards deteriorate below CLOUD NINE, and I hesitate to describe 2 3 4 and 5 but I hope dear reader that you will rise well above them. If you justify it.

As to activities on the Clouds there are many. We have Cherubims and Seraphims to delight us and best seats are reserved according to cloud formation. Under Cloud 5 it is almost impossible to be entertained.

Cherubims generally do little but look beautiful, and GOD frowns on interest other than platonic. There are several choirs of Seraphims who tend to sing in praise of GOD and little else. In this regard I am inclined to feel that he is a little unworldly, and life in the clouds could be enhanced somewhat by resort to a Top of the Pops culture on occasion.

At times residents are granted permission to view activities down below.

Wars seem to be quite popular, save that they do result in an unacceptable influx of newcomers not attuned to the ways of Heaven.

Grading them must be a nightmare and GOD generally delegates much of this to Jesus, John the Baptist et al. They are younger and more likely to understand the modern mind.

There are social evenings which I have been allowed to attend as a prospective occupier. I have sampled the food of the Gods which is a staple on these occasions and goes down well. As to drinks, for my own part I find Nectar a little too sweet, and though subject to a penalty point, have opted for a Gin and Tonic. The penalty point excluded me from the next Seraphim choir performance which I can live with.

There is a regular Quiz night which is extremely educational, and if I had the knowledge I have acquired here in such a short time, I feel sure that I would have advanced further in my chosen career.

The Quiz questions cover eras from 10000 B C to 2000 A D. Some of the participants are extremely impressive. Einstein is one, Old Moore another. There are several geniuses very willing to demonstrate their abundance of grey matter. Insufferable, some of them. Goodness me, I must conquer this unheavenly attitude if I mean to occupy part of CLOUD NINE.

Only the other day - possibly because I partook of two G & T's on the last Social Evening – I was reminded by one of the senior stewards – John the Baptist I believe, that it was open to the Committee, comprised in the main by those attending the Last Supper, and chaired by Jesus, that they had the power to relegate me to a lower cloud.

I take this very seriously, because I am sure I would settle well on CLOUD NINE and do not relish giving up a privileged place. Again, is this an unheavenly thought.

I cannot speak highly enough of the Duty Managers here. I would classify them as Trusties (not of course in the prison sense } and they man the Reception area 24/7. Always willing to respond to queries, to guide in the maintenance of accommodation, to advise on personal problems, and to initiate attention to any snags found on taking up residence. Provided that these are notified within 12 months.

My first three months in Limbo expired before I could fully adjust to the expectations of the Guardians of Cloud 9. However, as a result of a determined effort on my part, I was granted a further 3 months subject to a slight alteration in the site to be allocated to me on the cloud. In the event this caused me no problem. The admitting cherubims gave me support which I was pleased to acknowledge with a supply of 6 New Zealand Oyster Bay Sauvignon Blanc. Having done this I was overcome with the fear that a penalty point for a second gin & tonic (earlier, dear reader, of you are keeping abreast of the narrative) would easily be outstripped by penalties for this latest folly. I need not have worried because both Cherubims revealed a charming quality of human frailty which has endeared them to me, and

I have their word (and who can doubt the word of a Cherubim?) that they will keep schtum.

This, of course, is an Americanism for not grassing me up.

Admission is not guaranteed as yet but the signs are encouraging. I keep closely in touch with my favourite two cherubims.

They tell me that the main difficulty is that I am proving a little stubborn in being persuaded that I have reached the age at which most sensible people feel it right to move on to a higher plane. I have said that a few more disappointments down here (having to give up golf for example) will no doubt be a determining factor. It does occur to me that there is a problem, even in Heaven, with the demographics, wherein the population is more aged because of the modern world's ability to postpone the inevitable.

In any event I am given the impression that I must not be too tardy in case I lose my reservation which is so near my grasp. And that is on Cloud 9.

A DUTCH TALE

A STORY INSPIRED BY
ANTIQUE DELFT FIREPLACE TILES

16 TH 55

A
RESEARCH PROJECT

Prologue to a Dutch Tale

The tiles were produced in the 1600's onwards and stood proudly around a fireplace in a mansion of note. When that became derelict the tiles were moved to their new abode. They were presumably in chronological order and in part told a story of biblical significance, but it seems likely that they were installed in their new abode without due regard to this. Nor are the tiles only concerned with a religious story.

The aim of research and investigation was to explore this aspect, to date their manufacture and their places of origin(principally Delft, but not exclusively) and to clean up some of the images which, over time, have become less than clear and in some cases cracked. This has been done digitally but not of course physically because this would lead to further damage.

All the research and investigations have been carried out by John and Carol Young, as have the digital enhancements which have made the images so much clearer.They are to be congratulated on the work that they have done.

It was their suggestion that I might like to write a Dutch Tale about the tiles, and this is what follows. They have approved the less than serious approach I have adopted which in no way lessens my high regard for the real results their investigations have produced.

All the illustrations are by John Young and without them "A Dutch Tale" could not have been produced. I am indebted to him for the work he has done in this joint effort.

It requires no research to confirm that my interpretations of various tiles are rather silly. In defence can I say that in their raw state before enhancement, the interpretations of some were defensible, but with a clear view not so!

In any event I would not care for it to be thought that I am not aware that the work of the ancient tilers is remarkable and praiseworthy. My apologies to them if my ramblings cause any affront to the dignity of their work. Certainly this is not intended by me.

Let me introduce to you the family Van Klompf above.
Mijnheer Hannie and Mevrouw Gerda Van Klompf and
their only son young Hennie.

You will see their small house – later considerably increased in size – and strange to see the same 3 sail boats making little headway on the Zuider Zee, on the banks of which the Van Klompfs live.

Little Hennie was educated at home. You will see Hannie and little Hennie under a carob tree.

Hennie is being instructed in the mystery of Dutch agriculture. You will wonder at a carob tree in Holland, but such is the magic of the silt enriched soil that practically anything will grow and prosper, foreign or not. To add to the mystery it is found that the fruits of all the various trees around the Van Klompf residence, be they apple, orange, lemon, date, etc, when eaten and the pips spat out, produce a surprising result. I cannot find an illustration for this, but from the seeds, pips etc. of all the fruits, there springs one flower in many colours and of a shape and texture quite spectacular. Over time this has spread throughout thousands of acres, tourism has flourished because of them and the blooms are exported all over the world. What a pity I cannot point an example out, nor can I, for the life of me, bring to mind the name of this wonder. I do recall that some years ago an English singer called Max Bygraves gave it some publicity in old Amsterdam.

You will see the family home enlarged and the same 3 sail boats beating against the wind and not progressing. It may be that I am wrong in this assumption and what

I see is a regular commuter service to the City by 3 sail boats across the Zuider Zee, and depicted at the same time of day.

This illustration is instructive because it shows the first inhabitant of the Zuider Zee Zoolegen, established some years ago by a young couple. John Barrett was an Englishman who settled near Amsterdam and was entranced to meet Miss Holland of 1950, the Dutch representative in the Miss World competition. Her name was Elise Holland and so the title was appropriate.

Her heart was not really in it, and when John proposed, she was only too willing to move on, particularly as they had an all-consuming passion, -for each other naturally-and this passion extended over 40 years. It was John Barrett who memorably summed up his love for Elise by composing the song which goes: "We've been together naw for 40 years, and it don't seem a day too much. There ain't a lady living in the land as I'd swap for me dear old dutch. No there ain't a lady what's living in the land as I'd swap for me dear old dutch." Their other passion was for the animal kingdom and for the Holland and Barrett Zoolegen.

Why do I feel that Holland and Barrett have branched out of late? Certainly they derive a decent income from the sale of various oils, unctions, potions and pills, possibly sourced from their animals and these are said to cure many afflictions. Primrose oil springs to mind but this can hardly be from an animal source; possibly from the flower I still cannot put a name to. No No, it is not the primrose I am sure. Anyway, to join the story, the illustration shows a splendid stag, and you will also see Elise Barrett of Miss Holland fame, wrestling to the ground a large mountain goat before joining Zoolegen with the stag. You will also see the unusual strain of chicken above at the time of laying an egg and the strain is quite evident in the face.

Without doubt of course the most sensational creature to grace the Zoolegen is now the Zemeermin pictured here, very fetching in this study, but obviously quite vain in her preoccupation with the mirror which is always with her.

How she came to be in the Zoolegen is a story which bears telling.

Below can be seen a sailing boat near to the shore with three commuter boats in the background. We see its progress and it is too close to the shore for comfort, possibly as a result of the cannabis which the old sea dogs have smoked in celebration of what is a coup

indeed, for a Zemeermin is on board in a special glass tank and jealously guarded by her personal keeper appointed by the Captain. Unfortunately the poor seamanship which was borne of the intemperate manner of celebration was predictable in the outcome; the boat capsized and we see below some of the crew drying off. We have a mystery below also, because a would be rescuer has dived in to assist one of the crew who seems to be intent on putting him to the sword.

It turns out that the swordsman was the keeper assigned by the Captain to look after the welfare of the Zeemeermin during the journey. He was not happy at the thought that they might lose such a valuable asset which would provide a very good income from exhibiting their find. The intention was that they should approach the Holland and Barrett zoolegen for a contract to this end.

Nadia the Zeemeermin (for Nadia was her chosen name) came out of the shipwreck unscathed and found her way into one of the main canals, surfacing for a reconnaissance just as little Heinne was contemplating on the canal bank the increasing mysteries of life. At first he was frightened by the sudden appearance of Nadia as he had been at the appearance of a large and strange looking fish when he felt he was to partake of a fish meal - the meal to be Heinne.

On closer inspection he saw, not the vicious looking teeth he expected, but a pretty apparition seen below.

As the water was sufficiently clear, he had no doubt that he was seeing a real life Zeemeermin, until now unknown save in legend. Excited, he ran home to tell his parents and on the way came across Elise Barrett who listened to his story with interest, with great scepticism but with high regard for the imagination of the young boy.

She was disappointed later to learn that Heinne had been punished as shown. This was mainly because he had related the story to Elise for whom they had great respect, and did not appreciate that their son should pull her leg in this way. As to Nadia, she found the canal largely devoid of food which she could eat, and was intent on making her way back to the open sea. Unfortunately a sense of direction was not her strong point and she found herself next to the Van Klompf residence, now much improved as can be seen below, with the addition of a summer house in the grounds.

There is also a sizeable replica of a Mayan temple in Chichen Itza on the Yucatan peninsula. Why should Mexican history be celebrated by the Zuider Zee is anyone's guess but it was probably one of the mysteries being pondered by Heinne when he encountered the Zeemeermin a few lines back.

Nadia came across Heinne once again, and in some strange way was able to communicate with him well enough to understand that she would welcome some help. She had picked up a smattering of the Dutch language from shipwrecked mariners stranded on the rocks near her abode, all of whom perished when they were overwhelmed by the sea for a second time.

Heinnie felt it best now to enlist the help of Mevrouw Barrett, who quickly took command by guiding Nadia to the Zoolegen, fed her well, promised her comfort and reasonable freedom in the largest pool that could be constructed, with the company of dolphins (her favourite friends) and seals, also well favoured by Nadia. It was an appealing scenario into which the Zeemeermin settled well.

For their part John and Elise Barrett sought out the Captain, Nadia's keeper and the crew, all of whom had survived the shipwreck, and entered into a contract for fair division of the income from Nadia's fame.

Good friendships were established in the pool with the dolphins and seals, but there was something missing which would make a tremendous difference to the life of the Zeemeermin Nadia. We all know the soubriquet "a cold fish", but in Nadia's case that was a misnomer; she had a warm and lovable nature who would welcome a companion of her own kind who she could love, and was in little doubt that her feelings would be reciprocated. After all, she reasoned, the mirror does not lie.

Heinnie was a sensitive boy and had guessed that there was something lacking in Nadia's life and in one so young it was remarkable that he surmised correctly that mermen did exist, albeit in few numbers. He reasoned that the explosion of one myth relating to the existence of Zeemeermins must mean that the existence of Zeemeermen was not in doubt.

It was then that he recalled his unnerving experience and was able to construct a likeness which Nadia could interpret, and she immediately realised that Heinnie was showing her a soulmate.

Here was the typical merman of her girlish dreams, strong, large, with a ferocious appearance, but as she had learned in the distant past this was a cover for a gentle soul and merely a front to fend off any unwelcome attention by sharks and other predators.

Heinnie consulted Elise Barrett who was ready to listen to his idea of enticing the Zeemerman into the Zoolegen to join Nadia. Any scepticism she might have had was put to one side in her belief that this little boy was worth listening to when it came to fish. It was not going to be an easy enterprise but Heinne's idea of transporting Nadia to the Zuider Zee edge in a large water tank where she could be seen by the Zeemerman worked. The merman was nothing if not curious and it was a short time before both Nadia and Ajax (named by Nadia) were in the Zoolegen tank together. There was no animosity shown by the other occupants of the pool, who recognised Ajax for the big softie which he really was. They all settled to domestic bliss, and the public now had two myths exploded, for close examination of Ajax revealed a true merman.

Following these exciting events the Van Klompf family and the Barretts were welcomed at the Palace by Queen Wilhemina shown on her throne. At the celebrations to mark the amazing discoveries there was a programme of events; entertainments such as dance, orchestral works and drama.

A church service was held in thanksgiving in recognition of Heinnie's efforts in bringing the phenomenon of a pair of legendary sea creatures to the

world's attention, the Queen gave me the name of this national flower which has nagged at me throughout when she bestowed on him the Order of the Tulip. Primrose indeed!!!

An emblem at was affixed to the door of the Van Klompf residence to single it out as a home to someone of great importance.

That really is the end of the story, but there are other illustrations worthy of mention.

First there is a cannabis plant freely available in Amsterdam and elsewhere. Below can be seen 2 smokers

surfing the waves- a common occurrence after smoking cannabis I am told. Finally a wrestling match with an angel also popular with smokers.

It will come as no surprise to learn that young Heinnie concerned himself with the well being of the Zoolegen as he matured, and he learned a great deal from his close association with John and Elise Barrett who were happy to pass on to him all the animal husbandry wisdom which was at their command. In his turn Heinne became essential to their purpose which was to ensure the smooth running of the enterprise, and very soon he was in charge of the pool which was the major attraction of the business. This was an inspired appointment by the Barretts who recognised in Heinnie an affinity with all aquatic creatures. This was no better illustrated than by his increasing ability to communicate with Ajax and Nadia, and through them with some of the sharper dolphins and seals. The dolphins in particular were very intelligent, and in some situations acted as go betweens when communication between Heinnie and Ajax and Nadia were lost in the translation. As an aside it should be pointed out that Heinnie joined Dr.Doolittle in the unique ability to speak to the animals, although it must be said that the good Doctor had it over Heinnie in that he was able to reach most animals, and at this stage Heinnie restricted himself to his fish. But who knows what this remarkable boy might achieve in the future?

His parents were extremely proud of their son, and this was never more so than when he was made a Director of the Zoolegen at Zuider Zee at a very good salary, and with a substantial share of the profits generated by the pool and its attractions which were a magnet to the general public who came from far and wide.

This was Heinnie's overriding responsibility. Increasingly it prospered, and never more so than when Nadia let it be known (shyly it must be said) to Heinnie that they could shortly expect to hear the splash of tiny tails in the pool. Quadruplets were borne to Ajax and Nadia, two of each – Zeemeermin and Zeemeerman and this is likely to prove the founding of a dynasty in the Pool of the Zoolegen. The future of possible coupling by the offspring was not frowned upon in the aquatic world, and particularly when the paucity of partners was so restricted as in this case. Heinnie was at pains to point this out to his rather strict parents, who were at first disturbed at the prospect as explained by their son, but were so persuaded by Heinnie's arguments that they accepted the possibility, and in fact were impressed with the worldliness of their son. Rather surprised also that he should be conversant with the begetting of offspring in any species because he had been brought up with a complete blank slate so far as sexual content was concerned. They failed to realise that his connection with the animal world would provide all the education in this field which was required.

And so the story must end on the happy note that the Zoolegen at Zuider Zee is likely to be a fixture for many years to come; it will no doubt be Heinnie's future and we all wish him well. Who knows, we may come across him again in time to come.

THE PRINCESS
(A FAIRY TALE
NOT FOR
CHILDREN)

Once upon a time there lived a beautiful Princess, the only daughter of the King and Queen, brought into this world with love, and nurtured as a young girl with adoration by doting parents. At sixteen she was a vision of loveliness, and to embellish this with a nature of sweetness a veritable wonder to all. Her inner light was clear to those she met and charmed.

In herself she perceived none of this, being modest to a degree, and in the nature of young girls she dreamed of the coming of her handsome Prince to bring her alive as a woman and as a loving wife and helpmeet.

He came one day, handsome and silver tongued. It was a simple matter for him to conquer the innocence of the Princess with his talk of undying love, and she in turn felt she could return his love given time.

But in the nature of the worst of men his love was not true but merely lust, for he was not capable of any finer feeling. He seduced the Princess with force, traduced her, abused her until his desires were slaked like a thirst, and then cast her aside to a lower nobleman friend with the same evil ways.

Far away a distant Prince had been told of the lovely Princess, charmed by stories of her beauty, of her modesty, of her generosity of spirit. He set out to shorten the distance between them and time sped by until, eventually, he came upon her in her father's Kingdom.

He found a pitiful young girl, harrowing in her appearance and with her inner light all but extinguished. He was enraged to learn of her treatment by the other Prince and his henchman, and in his true noble spirit tracked down both and killed them in duels. He was well aware that in a parody of justice he would be found guilty of unlawful killing and could face the hangman's noose, accepting that the law was an ass but the law nevertheless.

He returned to the Princess and in a very short time came to see beyond her shell the same loveliness, modesty and charm spoken about when he first knew of her existence. In turn she responded to his great kindness, and between them grew true love. The Princess recognised this with wonder. Both knew that this love could be cut short by the intervention of "justice" and both agreed that they would not allow separation.

The Prince sought out a potion, and together they laid down and drank deeply.

The next day the King and Queen found them in each other's arms, the Princess with her beauty fully restored, and both with an expression of deep happiness.

A note was left asking that they be married forthwith; a Priest was summoned, the ceremony celebrated with joy, and the couple died happily ever after.

About the Author

Alan Gibbins, retired Bank Manager, now 89, took to writing short stories recently.

This is his first publication.

Lightning Source UK Ltd.
Milton Keynes UK
UKOW07f0317030616

275527UK00008B/17/P